AF578135

HOLDING ONTO COURAGE

A Novel

By

Kelly Flanagan

HOLDING ONTO COURAGE
2nd Edition
Copyright © 2024 by Kelly Flanagan

All rights reserved. No part of this book may be reproduced or transmitted in any form or by any means without written permission of the author and publisher.

This is a work of fiction. Any resemblance to actual persons, living or dead, is purely coincidental.

ISBN: 9798991537223

Library of Congress Control Number: 2024951968

Cover Design by All Things that Matter Press

Published in 2024 by All Things that Matter Press

To all my former students—avid readers and those still searching for the book that inspires them—I hope you always experience the joy and wonder that comes from reading a great book.

1 ~ The Fight
2024

Kim glared at her dad before throwing herself across the bed, burying her head in the puffy pillows piled against the headboard. "I'm not going," she wailed.

Not hearing any response, Kim looked up, her dark hair clinging to her damp face. Her dad stood next to the bed, hands planted on his hips and face turning an angry shade of red. She sat up, clenching her fists like a boxer ready for a fight. Hot tears tunneled down, catching along the curve of her lip. "I can't let my team down when we made the playoffs."

Her dad threw up his hands. "This is the trip of a lifetime. It means so much to Grandma Mai for you to learn about your heritage. You will go."

Kim lowered her arms but threw a defiant look at him. Each hiccuppy breath echoed off the walls of the room. "I was excited to go to Vietnam when we talked about it a few months ago, but things changed. I want to stay home and play soccer."

"Kim," Dad pleaded. "We've been planning this trip for months. Grandma's been dreaming about returning to Vietnam ever since she got that cancer scare last year. She hasn't been back since moving here forty-six years ago."

Standing up, Kim turned toward her dad. She was desperate for him to understand why canceling the trip was so important. Grandma Mai could take her trip next year. "If we get through the playoffs and make it to the championship, I might be selected for the National Youth Soccer Team. It's my dream."

"And what about Grandma's dream?" Dad said. He turned and stalked out of the room.

After her dad left, Kim sat on the bed, sniffing back tears. It was so unfair. All year, she worked hard to improve her game. Her team only lost once this season, and the playoffs looked promising. She could take her team to the championship—if she didn't have to take time off for a trip to Vietnam.

Kim heard her parents talking in the living room, her dad's voice rising and her mom's voice gently responding. Hope replaced the despair that was anchored in her chest. Mom had a way of calming her dad, no matter why he was mad. Maybe they were talking about postponing the trip? They had to understand how much being in the playoffs meant to her.

The house grew quiet, and, after a while, Kim's mom entered the bedroom, carrying a basket of laundry. She plopped the basket on the bed next to Kim, handed her a shirt to fold, and began sorting socks.

Kim rolled her eyes. "You think that folding laundry solves all problems." It seemed that it was always while folding laundry that Kim shared her hopes and worries with her mom. Not having Mom looking at her made it easier to talk.

Her mom smiled as she tossed another shirt at Kim. "It's very calming, isn't it?" They folded laundry as they talked. "Grandma Mai never wanted to return to Vietnam. She always said the time wasn't right. It's strange how Grandma and Aunt Lang never talk about their life there or why they came to the United States."

Kim nodded. She hadn't thought about it before, but it was true.

"Now, Grandma is excited to show you how she grew up and where she lived."

Looking into her mom's eyes, Kim willed her to understand. "But Mom, I'll miss the playoffs."

"You'll be back home before the championship."

Kim stood up and angrily kicked her soccer ball against the wall. "I'm pretty sure Coach won't let me play in the championship if I miss the playoff games."

When she saw the disappointment on her mom's face, Kim softened. Her mom watched while Kim passed the soccer ball between her feet. Then, she kicked it into the air and caught it in her hands. "Maybe you, Dad, and Grandma can go to Vietnam without me?"

Her mom frowned. "Dad and Grandma Mai want you to learn about Vietnam. After all, you are half-Vietnamese."

Kim sighed. "You don't understand. I don't care about where Grandma grew up or how she lived. Mom, I'm surprised you care, since you aren't Vietnamese. I love Grandma Mai, but what happened in Vietnam almost fifty years ago doesn't matter."

Mom pleaded with her. "Kim, this trip is important."

Squeezing her ball in frustration, Kim sighed. "You don't need me to come with you. Dad and Grandma can explore Vietnam together. It will be a great mother/son adventure, and I'll hear all about it when you return."

It seemed like the time in Grandma Mai's life when she lived in Vietnam made her sad. Their family still celebrated holidays with Vietnamese food, like hu tieu, a brothy pork soup with shrimp served over rice and noodles. They even followed some Vietnamese traditions like welcoming the new year by receiving a red envelope full of money, but Grandma Mai never shared any personal stories.

Besides including a few Vietnamese traditions in their holiday celebrations, Kim knew very little about Vietnam. Grandma was a closed book and Kim was more interested in fitting in with her friends than learning about things that set her apart.

Shrugging her shoulders, Kim dropped the soccer ball to the ground and grabbed her cell phone off the dresser. Shooting a final look at her mom, who never let her kick her soccer ball in the house, she dribbled out the door, through the open living room and out the back door.

2 ~ The Next Football Star 1975

Mai Kien stood outside a dingy two story building, scanning the crowded street in Ho Chi Minh City. "Lang, where are you?" she muttered. Their father didn't like it when Lang went off by herself.

Vendors stood behind wooden carts on the street. One cart was full of bright pink dragonfruit, spiky durian, and deep purple passion fruit. Another was loaded with silvery fish, their eyes still bulging. Other carts held silken shirts, wooden bowls, and leather sandals. Mai's stomach gurgled. She was so busy helping customers in their family pharmacy that she didn't have time to eat lunch.

People gathered around the booths or hurried down the sizzling sidewalks on their way to stores or their apartments. Cars, bikes and rickshaws filled the street. The shouts of vendors rose above the hum of traffic and barking dogs.

Mai spotted Lang in the small grassy park across the street and she exhaled in relief. With a tiny nose and heart-shaped face, Lang looked like a mini-Mai. She was passing a black and white football between her feet. The hexagons on the ball seemed to spin as it moved faster and faster.

Even though the war ended months ago, it still felt unsafe for a young girl to be outside alone, especially one who was more interested in dribbling a football than in her surroundings. "Lang, come quickly. Ba is looking for you," she yelled through cupped hands.

Seeing Lang pick up the football and head toward the pharmacy, Mai turned, bumping right into a North Vietnamese soldier. His dark green pith helmet sat low on his forehead, and he gripped a rifle. "Get out of my way," he muttered before striding down the street. She shuddered, knowing it was best to avoid the soldiers patrolling the area.

Through the window, Mai saw an older woman standing at the counter, balancing on a cane with both hands. She walked back into the pharmacy and picked up a small brown bottle from behind the counter. "Here are the pills you needed, Mrs. Pham. My father said to take one pill right before bedtime." The tiny woman clutched the bottle, bowed delicately and exited right as Lang rushed in.

"Mai, is it time for the football game?" Lang dropped her ball and grabbed a duffel bag from behind the counter.

A few years ago, Coach Huang, a former professional football player, started a casual football league for kids in Ho Chi Minh City to distract them from the war. He organized both boys and girls into ragtag teams, and if they were lucky, they occasionally played a game at Vinhomes Central Park.

Glancing at her watch, a wave of irritation overcame Mai. "Yes, it's time." Since the North Vietnamese took control of South Vietnam at the end of the Vietnam War, Ba needed her to work in the pharmacy instead of going to school. She wished she were ten, like Lang, instead of fifteen, so she could just go to school and play football.

Mai pushed her bangs away and flipped her long, fat braid over her shoulder. Removing the white apron that covered her *ao dai,* the colorful tunic reaching just above her knees, Mai called to her father. "Ba, it's time for Lang's football game. Are you coming or do you want me to take her?"

Looking up from the bottles of pills he was counting, Ba gave a weary smile. "Can you go without me? We're so busy that I'll have to work into the night just to fill prescriptions."

Mai was about to answer, when she heard Lang impatiently shouting from the front door. "I can't be late."

Lang dashed out the door, duffel bag slung over her shoulder and football tucked in the crook of her arm. Mai followed, blinking in the bright sunlight as they set off down the sidewalk. The humid air was filled with the smell of tasty *Bun cha,* spicy meatballs, ginger and fresh cilantro. As she walked, Mai alternated between watching Lang who was skipping ahead and the soldiers standing on the street corners. During the war, people stayed close to home. Now, crowds filled the streets, but they still avoided the soldiers.

Although dingy, buildings stood tall and proud. Surprisingly, Ho Chi Minh sustained very little damage during the war. The air force base was destroyed, and some buildings were damaged by errant shells, but mostly, the city looked the same as it did before the war. Most of the fighting took place in rural areas to the north. The biggest change was that the city was renamed from Saigon to Ho Chi Minh, after a famous communist leader.

Lang stopped at the street corner. "Hurry up, Mai."

Mai caught up and playfully tugged on the strap of Lang's duffel bag. "Impatient, aren't we? Today was very busy and I had to take time to come find you."

Lang rolled her eyes. "It's always busy. Come out and have some fun sometimes."

Mai frowned. Lang wasn't old enough to understand the impact the war had on them. Where Lang still went to school, played soccer, and spent time with friends, Mai was expected to act like an adult. It wasn't fair.

"Just because you want to be a pro football player someday doesn't mean you're in charge now," Mai kidded.

Lang laughed, turned the corner, and skipped down the sidewalk ahead of Mai. "If I were in charge, kids would have real football leagues and Vietnamese women would be allowed to play on professional teams."

Mai walked faster to keep up with Lang. She wished that would be true. Lang was a talented football player. Coming to the entrance to Vinhomes Central Park, Lang dropped the ball to the ground, kicked it high into the air, and then caught it with the top of her other foot.

She turned toward Mai. "Someday, I will be a pro football player. It's my dream." Then Lang ran off to join her team.

And what about my dreams, Mai thought.

3 ~ It's Hard to be Kim 2024

Kim knew exactly what she needed to do—talk to her best friends, Charlotte and Mason, about the fight with her parents. They would understand. After quick texts to them, they agreed to meet her at the park around the corner from her house.

Since the July afternoon was hot and humid, the playground was empty except for two kids building a sandcastle. Kim pulled the phone from her pocket and plopped down on the merry-go-round. The three of them met on the same playground when they were in kindergarten. Now, it was still their go-to place whenever they wanted to just hang out and talk.

Looking up from her phone, Kim saw Mason approaching first. He lifted his hand in a half wave. Mason was the serious one in the group. His gray-rimmed glasses constantly slid down his nose which made him look both dope and geek at the same time, if that was possible.

He sat next to her on the merry-go-round, long legs planted firmly on the ground. "Hey, what's up?"

"It's my mom and dad. Sometimes they drive me crazy." Kim started to say more, but stopped when she spotted Charlotte jogging over. Charlotte's curly red hair made her easy to spot. Everyone noticed her strawberry hair, sprinkles of freckles across her nose, and crooked smirk. She was bubbly, funny, and a loyal friend.

Charlotte sat down cross-legged on the other side of Kim. "Okay, what's wrong?"

Kim's shoulders slumped. "You know how I told you a few months ago that we were going on vacation to Vietnam? Well, we're going. Next week."

Charlotte and Mason looked at each other, with confused expressions. "Umm. So what's the problem?" Charlotte said.

Kim looked at them, incredulous. "I can't believe you forgot the playoffs are next week. I've been talking about them ever since soccer season started." She felt a lump rising in her throat and swallowed hard so she wouldn't cry.

Mason jumped off the merry-go-round and gave it a gentle push so it slowly turned. "I'd give anything to travel to a foreign country and you'll be back in time for the championship."

Charlotte nodded.

Head bent in despair; Kim tried to explain. "I'm worried that if I don't play in the playoffs, Coach won't let me be in the championship."

Mason thought a minute. "I know you've worked hard this season so your team could get to the playoffs. Can your parents talk to your coach?"

"It's more than that," Kim said. "I haven't told Mom and Dad, but you know Jayna's been giving me a hard time on and off the soccer field. A few others joined in. If I leave, it gives her more time to turn the team against me."

Kim told them a few of the things Jayna did. Last week, her shin guards turned up missing from her duffel bag. Coach wouldn't let her practice without them, so she had to sit on the bench the entire practice. After practice, a smiling Jayna handed the missing shin guards to her. She claimed she found them under the bench. Another time, Jayna refused to pass the ball to Kim the entire practice. There would be an open shot right to her, and Jayna would look past her and pass to another teammate. It always happened when Coach was at the other end of the field or talking to a parent.

Charlotte put her hand on Kim's arm. "That's awful. I didn't know Jayna had a mean streak. Now I understand. It would be impossible to play in the Championship when your entire team is against you. Of course, you can't go to Vietnam."

Kim knew Charlotte would back her up. No matter what, Charlotte always sided with her. Mason usually thought things through before speaking. He sat down next to Kim and pushed his glasses up, a habit he had whenever he was deep in thought.

"Do you think Jayna is still mad at you from last year or could it be something else?"

Kim sighed. "I'm not sure."

Last year, Kim's team also made the playoffs. In the final minutes of the last playoff game, the score was tied. Kim was dribbling the ball down the field, ready to pass it to Jayna, who would drive it in for the winning goal. In a surprise move, Kim decided to do an outside kick to Jayna. Unfortunately, something went horribly wrong. Instead of the ball being passed cleanly, it wobbled down the field straight to an awaiting foot on the opposing team. They quickly took the ball down the field and scored the winning goal. Kim was embarrassed and devastated, her team was disappointed, and Jayna was beyond angry.

Kim folded her knees to her chest and pressed her forehead against them. She just wanted to forget about the trip, the bullying, and the pressure to redeem herself after last year.

"Maybe you should talk to your coach?" Mason said.

Kim looked up. "It's so frustrating. He doesn't see what Jayna does to me because she's so sneaky. I don't think he'd believe me."

Mason nodded. "Have you told your parents about Jayna? Maybe they would agree to cancel the trip then?"

"Dad said he won't cancel the trip. He says Grandma Mai really wants me to go. And if I told them I was being bullied, they would never let me stay back while they went." She felt like the rope in a game of tug-a-war. "Maybe I should just go."

Charlotte looked at Kim, her eyebrows arching in surprise. "Are you crazy? You can't just let a bully win. And these are the playoffs. You even told me it's your chance to shine. My best friend could be selected for the national team. You absolutely can't go."

Even Mason agreed. "This changes things," he said. "You can't run away from a bully. You need to stay and fight."

Kim smiled. She felt better just talking to them. "You're right. I can't go on that trip to Vietnam. Now, how do I convince my parents?"

4 ~ It's Hard to be Hoa 1977

Two years passed since the end of the war and life changed for the Kien family. Mai still worked in the pharmacy every day, Lang spent hours playing football with friends, and the sidewalk was still filled with vendors, but Mai was worried.

On a very quiet Saturday, Mai and her father worked side by side, stocking shelves. "Ba, I don't understand. Last year, we were too busy. Why aren't people shopping here anymore? I know they need medicine, but they pass by our store."

Setting a heavy box down, Ba sat on it with a thump. His hair seemed to have turned from a rusty black to a silvery gray overnight. He exhaled loudly and motioned for Mai to sit beside him. She turned over the wooden box she finished unpacking and sat down.

"We're Hoa and I'm proud of that," he began. "The Hoa, like your grandparents, were successful businesspeople who immigrated from China."

"I remember your story," Mai said excitedly. "Your parents, my *Ông nội* and *Bà nội,* moved from China and started an ice cream shop right here. When I was little, I loved sitting at the counter, eating ice cream with them."

Ba grinned at the memory. "I added a pharmacy that you'll run when you're older."

Mai looked out the huge picture window facing the bustling street. "Ba, what does being Hoa have to do with people passing by without coming in? Sometimes I even see them peer through the window with angry faces."

She shivered as she thought of the scowls on people who used to be their customers and friends.

Ba looked at Mai, his face crinkled with sadness. "When the communist government gained control over South Vietnam, they took shops away from their owners. People lost their jobs and homes. Everyone is very poor now, except the Hoa. They allowed us to keep our businesses because China will still trade with the Hoa."

"Do people hate us because we still have money?" Mai asked.

"Yes. It's hard for our neighbors to see that we still have what they don't. And the soldiers are angry because we own a business when communists believe the government should own all businesses."

"But we didn't take our neighbor's jobs away," Mai said.

It was complicated and Mai wasn't sure she understood. It seemed like people in Ho Chi Minh were divided into two groups - the Hoa and all other Vietnamese people. Their heart-shaped faces and angled eyebrows made the Hoa look slightly different than native people, but weren't they all Vietnamese?

Leaning back against an empty shelf, Ba wrapped his arms around himself, as if that shut out the evil in the world. His slumped shoulders and silvery hair made him look old.

Mai paced around the store, anger and fear clutching her like icy fingers. "Do you think we'll lose our pharmacy? Should we leave Vietnam?"

Ba rubbed his hands together, something he did whenever he was worried. "Others are leaving. Business owners, former soldiers in the South Vietnamese army, and people who worked for the U.S. government are leaving for Europe, Australia, and the United States instead of being sent to re-education camps, but I am going to do everything I can to stay."

Mai looked around the empty store. Even the few customers who entered quickly purchased what they needed and left. Before, they would stay to chat. She was troubled that their customers, who were friends and neighbors, were afraid to be around them. It made Mai nervous to leave the safety of her home.

Last evening, when she left the store to walk with Lang to the park, a North Vietnamese soldier stepped in front of her and mumbled, "Filthy Hoa." People heard and looked away. And a neighbor actually spit at her feet when she passed him. Mai looked straight ahead and walked through it all, but her face burned in embarrassment.

Ba walked over to the window next to Mai. Pushcarts full of fresh fish and steamy pho soup were set up across the street from their store. A beggar stood between the carts, arms outstretched, asking for food or coins. Two boys in ragged pants and oversized shirts sold litchi nuts on the corner.

Mai was startled. She never paid attention, but now realized there were so many people struggling to survive. "Ba, I think we're lucky to still have a store and home. It isn't fair that so many are suffering, but it also isn't fair that our neighbors blame us." She felt mixed up inside.

Her father nodded. "Now you understand why they are angry. We still have our shop ... for now." Glancing at his watch, Ba said, "I'm glad that Lang still has football games to keep her busy. Let's close the pharmacy early and we'll take her together."

Mai really wanted to curl up with a book and cup of tea, but she felt obligated to come. Safety in numbers. Lang and football. Some things don't change, Mai thought.

5 ~ The Compromise 2024

Kim was in the backyard, practicing her outside kick. The argument with her dad was forgotten while she focused on soccer. Over and over, she ran up to the waiting ball and slammed it with the outside of her foot. Each time, the ball wobbled and landed short of the makeshift net.

Frustrated, Kim wiped the sweat from her forehead and leaned against a tree to rest. She looked away from the sun burning in the cerulean sky. *Quiet, so quiet,* Kim thought. Even the birds nested silently in the shade instead of singing their high-pitched songs. She wished there was even a little breeze. After taking a few minutes to cool down, she returned to practicing.

Next door, Aunt Lang stood on a leaning wooden deck. She wore a silk tunic and baggy white pants. Deep lines etched her face. Grandma Mai and Great Aunt Lang, her younger sister, lived together in the tiny yellow house next to Kim's family. Where Mai was kind, gentle and happy, Lang was dour, loud and angry.

Kim lived next door to Grandma and Aunt Lang her whole life. Lang always seemed to find the dark cloud in a silver lining, but in the last few years, she grew even more critical. What made her such a sad, bitter person? Like Grandma Mai, Lang never talked about her past.

Each time Kim kicked the ball, Lang rubbed her hands together and looked upward, irritation spreading across her pinched face. "You will never get better if you keep repeating the same mistake over and over," she shouted. Lang's accent made her enunciate each word as if it were a separate sentence.

Kim ignored her hurtful jab and tried an outside kick again. Lang crossed the deck and marched to the edge of her yard. "Kim, that kick is worse than a two-year-old trying to kick a beach ball. Each day, I watch, and you never get any better," she grumbled. "Maybe you should find a new sport."

Exasperated, Kim glared at her. "Leave me alone. It doesn't help to tell me how bad I am." Even to herself, Kim sounded disrespectful, but Aunt Lang brought out the worst in her. Kim strode toward Lang. She was consumed by anger. Anger at losing last year's playoffs for the team. Anger at having to choose between soccer and traveling to Vietnam. Anger at having this mean, critical person as her aunt.

She stood in front of Lang. "Stop watching me. Stop telling me that I'm not very good. You don't know anything about soccer." Her ponytail bounced in rhythm to the words she spit out.

Aunt Lang's eyes narrowed into angry slits. Her lips quivered and she looked like she was about to cry. "Maybe I don't, but maybe I do." Then she walked back into her house.

Kim gave her soccer ball a hard kick. It sailed over a low bush and landed in the flower garden. Then she stomped into her own house.

Mom, Dad and Grandma Mai were talking at the wooden table that filled their tiny dining room. Listening from the kitchen, Kim caught random words from their muffled conversation. Vietnam. Soccer. Playoffs. She felt hopeful. Kim crossed the kitchen and stood in the doorway to the dining room. "Are you talking about the trip?"

The conversation stopped and three heads turned toward her. Dad looked annoyed, his arms crossed, and lips pursed. He motioned for her to come in. Kim sat in the chair across from Grandma Mai, studying her face for a sign if they decided to postpone the trip. Her lips curved slightly upward, but it was hard to read her. Grandma always seemed content.

Tension filled the room. Grandma Mai absentmindedly adjusted the necklace tucked under her blouse. The fine gold chain hung from her neck, but the rest of the necklace remained hidden under her shirt, as always. When she was little, Kim asked about the necklace. Grandma Mai sighed and didn't talk for a long time. Kim was curious, but didn't want to make her grandma sad, so she never asked again.

Dad and Mom shot each other "that look." Kim sighed. It meant they agreed with each other on some big decision that she wouldn't like. She wanted to just walk back out but wasn't willing to risk her parents' reaction if she did.

"Our trip to Vietnam was planned months ago. You have your passport. I already paid for the plane tickets." Dad began. "I know that soccer is important to you, and we support your passion, but taking a three-week trip won't ruin your soccer career."

Kim's heart sank and tears gathered at the edge of her eyes. Disappointment sat in her throat like an apple wedge that wouldn't descend. She knew she lost the battle but tried one more time. "After last year's bad end to the season, I just want the chance to do well in the playoffs. I need to prove to myself I can do it, and I can't if I'm in Vietnam." They were at a standstill. Mom and Dad against her, and Kim knew she would lose.

Grandma Mai stood and cleared her throat to get the family's attention. "Kim has a good point. I think she should be allowed to stay back. I don't want her to miss such a great opportunity."

Dad harrumphed and leaned back in his chair. Mom placed her hand on Dad's arm. "Tran, Kim is young. There will be other opportunities for her to go to Vietnam. I agree with Mai."

"There will be other opportunities for soccer playoffs too," her dad said.

Kim stared at the ground. She didn't want to say anything to mess things up now. After all, Mom and Grandma switched to her side. When Grandma spoke, her voice was soft and sad. "A long time ago, I got in the way of someone's dream. I refuse to do that again."

It was quiet for a moment and then Dad nodded. "If you are okay with Kim staying home, then I will agree."

Kim reached out to give Grandma Mai a hug, but Mai held out the palm of her hand, like a stop sign. "There is one condition, though. I want Kim to stay with Lang. I've talked to Lang and she agreed to watch Kim."

In a matter of seconds, Kim's feelings changed from joy to disbelief. How could Grandma think that staying with grumpy Aunt Lang was a good idea? She plastered a smile on her face. "Deal." It was going to be a long three weeks.

6 ~ Unwanted 1977

Mai opened the door that led from the store to their upstairs apartment. "Lang, time for your game."

Usually, Lang bounded down the stairs when it was time for a game. Today, she took each step slowly, ball in one hand and duffel bag hanging from her slumped shoulders.

"We'll stay and watch your game today," Ba said.

Lang drew in a breath. "No, I, um, I'm distracted when you watch." There was a touch of panic in her voice.

Mai laughed. "Since when do you even notice we're there?"

Shrugging, Lang headed out the door with Mai and Ba following. When they approached a soldier on the corner, Lang lowered her head and crossed the street to avoid him. Mai noticed but wasn't surprised. After all, she tried her hardest to avoid the soldiers, too.

After arriving at the park, Lang walked to the edge of the field where a group of boys and girls gathered. Mai and her father sat in the bleachers. The kids were wearing the t-shirts Coach Huang gave them when he formed the teams. Their name and number were written on the back of the shirt using a black marker. Even though they weren't an official team, they could still have a makeshift uniform.

When Coach Huang blew his whistle, the kids ran out on the field, laughing and passing the ball back and forth to each other. Mai noticed everyone ran by Lang as she trudged onto the field, almost like she was invisible. Puzzled, Mai watched Lang more closely. "Something is wrong."

Last week, Lang complained about some kids on the team who didn't like her. Mai brushed off Lang's complaints as typical friend drama. Now, she wasn't so sure. When the game began, Lang ran down the field, just ahead of the ball. When the football sailed past her, Lang raised her foot to stop it. Just as she did, her teammate, Cam, ran by and kicked the ball away from her. Mai gasped as she watched Cam say something to Lang and continue down the field. Lang froze in place for a moment, scowling, but then recovered and joined her team.

During halftime, Lang stood off to the side while her team gathered on a bench. Wanting to make sure Lang was okay, Mai left the bleachers and joined her. "They're being so mean to you and Coach Huang isn't doing anything about it."

Lang slammed her ball down. "I told you not to come. They ignore me because I'm Hoa. Coach Huang sees it, but said if he tries to stop it, the other players will quit. Let me handle this." Lang ran off to join her team.

Mai stood there, surprised that Lang was angry with her. She debated what to do, when she felt Ba's hand on her shoulder. "I see what's happening. We can't help Lang, and she doesn't want to quit."

To Mai, it seemed like they were giving in if they let her teammates get away with it. She started to argue, but Ba motioned for her to stay quiet. He moved closer to where the team gathered for a water break. He didn't say anything, but Mai watched his piercing stare at the players, as if warning them to leave Lang alone. When the game started again, he wagged his outstretched index finger at them as a reminder that a respected elder was watching.

Sometimes teammates nudged Lang or stole the ball, but it happened less often. Mai stood next to Ba, seething. She was angry at Lang's team, frustrated Lang just took their treatment, and disappointed Ba wasn't doing more to stop them. Mai knew she would have walked off the field ten minutes into the game.

"Ba, why doesn't Lang just quit?"

"Lang wants to play football. I'm proud of her determination."

When the game ended with Lang's team winning, she walked over to Cam, the girl who pushed her down. Until today, Mai thought they were best friends. Thinking back, Mai realized Lang mostly hung out by herself the past few months and friends never came over anymore. She moved close enough to the sideline to hear Lang's conversation with Cam.

Lang's voice was like cold steel. "What have I done for you to treat me like this? I understand why we are no longer friends, but do you have to be so cruel?"

Cam stared at the ground and remained silent. Lang stood tall, making her look fearless. The silence was broken by Coach Huang calling the team over. A man in a beige safari jacket holding a professional camera stood beside him. Coach high-fived the players and handed them a first place ribbon. Then he pointed to the man beside him. "Mr. Nguyen is a newspaper reporter. He is writing an article about my football league. Your picture is going to be in the paper."

The kids lined up in rows, each holding up a ribbon and smiling. Lang stood at the edge of the first row, with a forced smile. The reporter snapped the picture, and everyone ran off.

Mai joined Lang, wrapping an arm around her. "How long has this been going on?"

Lang looked at the ground, avoiding Mai's stare. "Months. I thought it would get better if I just ignored it. They hate me because I'm Hoa. I tried to tell you and Ba, but both of you were so worried about the store and I didn't want to add to your problems."

"You need to quit. Nobody should be treated how they treat you."

Lang backed away. "That's why I didn't want you and Ba to come. I want to play football and quitting would give them what they want. Ever since Ba took us to see Australia play in the South Vietnam National Day tournament when I was four, I've wanted to play football. I'm not quitting."

Mai and Lang didn't see Ba standing near them until he spoke. "Lang, you are a fighter. You are fierce and loyal. Show them that a Hoa can't be bullied into leaving." He put his arm around her and the three of them walked home.

7 ~ The Mystery of Lang
2024

Kim stretched as she sat up in bed. Beams of sunshine sparkled through the window and made triangular patterns on the floor. She heard urgent voices outside her bedroom, but she curled under her soft quilt for a few more minutes.

The last week was stressful with Dad maintaining a stony silence and Mom acting extra cheerful. Aunt Lang was just plain crabby, giving the impression she felt the same as Kim about spending three long weeks together. The only person who acted normal was Grandma Mai. She talked animatedly about the trip, gave Lang a thousand instructions on how to take care of the house while they were gone, and teased Dad about being grumpy.

Grandma Mai knocked on Kim's bedroom door and then walked in without waiting for a response. Typical. "Wake up, sleepyhead. Today's an exciting day. A trip for me and playoffs for you."

"Oh, Grandma Mai. I'm glad you finally get to go to Vietnam. I never knew you wanted to go back." Kim hopped out of bed and gave her a hug. "Thank you for understanding that I want to stay here."

Grandma Mai sat on the bed. "For years, I didn't want to return to Vietnam. There were so many bad memories. It was a hard decision, but it's time to think about the good memories and I really want your dad to see the country where he was born."

Kim didn't ask about the bad memories. This was a happy day for Grandma. "I'm excited for you, but did you really have to insist I stay with cranky Aunt Lang? Charlotte and Mason said I could stay at their houses."

"There is more to Lang than what you see," Grandma Mai said cryptically.

"Huh?" Kim started to ask what she meant, but Grandma gave her another quick hug and left the room.

Kim wasn't sure which was worse, missing playoffs to go to Vietnam or spending three weeks with Aunt Lang. Shrugging, she decided that being in the playoffs was worth dealing with a mean old aunt.

After slipping into her blue and gold soccer uniform, Kim bounded down the hallway, stopping at her parents' bedroom. Two huge suitcases overflowing with clothes covered their bed. Her mom looked up and laughed. "Kim, help me close my suitcase. It looks like I packed for three months instead of three weeks."

Kim plopped her butt on top of the suitcase and her mom clicked the levers that closed it. She felt a twinge of regret and nervousness. Maybe she should tell her parents about Jayna? No. Not the right time. She took a gulp of air, and with it, her confidence returned. "I'm going to miss you, Mom."

Her mom studied Kim's face. "Are you okay?"

Kim smiled. "Yeah. I hope you, Dad, and Grandma have a great time."

After leaving her mom's bedroom, Kim spied Grandma sitting next to an even larger suitcase in the living room, her thin hand clutching the handle. Aunt Lang and Grandma Mai were so deep in conversation, they didn't notice her.

"Lang, I wish you were coming," Grandma said.

Aunt Lang gritted her teeth, spitting out each word. "Why would I want to go back to a country that did not want us?"

Mai stared at her, pleading with her eyes. "Things have changed. The Vietnamese people no longer hate us. We had many beautiful memories there as we grew up, and I miss the bustling city and seashore."

Lang's face turned red, and she pursed her lips. "Our trip from Vietnam to America is full of bad memories. Never again do I want to think about it, let alone return to a country that destroyed my life."

Mai hesitated before speaking, as if deciding what to say. "Our life here has been good. You chose what to do with your life once we arrived. Do you now have regrets?"

"We've had this discussion many times. I don't want to talk about it anymore."

"Please be happy for me," Grandma begged.

Kim felt like she was spying on Grandma and Lang, but they had to know she was in the room. Vietnam destroyed Lang's life? How? She was confused, but didn't want to interrupt such a serious conversation. Kim decided to quietly leave. Turning, she bumped against the bookcase, causing her to drop her soccer ball. The thud of it hitting the wooden floor and rolling across the room startled all three of them. Grandma and Lang stopped their conversation and looked at her.

Aunt Lang stood up. "Are you ready to leave for your soccer game?" she asked.

Kim nodded and gave Grandma Mai a final hug. "I hope you have a great trip."

Lang sighed and wrapped her arms around Mai. "If returning to Vietnam brings you peace, then I am happy you are going."

Kim gave her mom and dad a fierce hug as they rolled their suitcases to the door and told them how much she would miss them. Then, she and Aunt Lang were off.

Lang got in the driver's seat of her ancient Chevrolet Spark and Kim hopped into the passenger side. Kim talked animatedly about plans for the week and her hard work at soccer practice. Aunt Lang drove in silence. She couldn't wait to show Aunt Lang how much she improved her outside kick.

As they got closer to the soccer field, it seemed like a gray cloud appeared above Lang's head. She was sullen and mumbled complaints under her breath. Kim stopped talking and worry invaded her thoughts, like a shadowy figure trespassing in her mind. Usually, her parents joked and gave her a pep talk on the way to her games. She wasn't used to silence.

Kim decided that any conversation was better than the quiet. "I'm excited for you to see my game."

Silence.

Kim's thoughts turned to Jayna. She wished she had told her parents about Jayna before they left. They would know what to do. It was too late for that. More brooding silence. Kim gave up. She took out her phone and texted Charlotte and Mason. They would calm her nerves. Lang pulled up to the gate surrounding the soccer field and stopped. Kim sat there in disbelief. "Aren't you going to watch my game?" She just expected that with her parents gone, Lang would come.

Lang gave a curt nod. "I don't want to waste my time. I will be back to pick you up after the game."

Kim frowned and turned her head. She didn't want Lang to have the satisfaction of seeing she was upset. Grabbing her duffel bag, she opened the car door and slipped out. Anger, confusion, disbelief, anticipation for the game. She felt so many emotions. Lang hated soccer ever since Kim knew her. Even if she didn't like the sport, why was she so hurtful and mean? It was a mystery.

8 ~ The Final Straw 1977

Over and over, Mai begged Lang to quit football. "Your teammates either shove you or ignore you. Lang, you're going to get injured. Don't you care?"

"I do care." Lang balled her hands into fists, her face red and eyes blazing. "I hate being taunted or ignored. But it won't always be this way, and until then, I want to play football."

Mai threw up her hands, exasperated that Lang just accepted how they treated her. "What do you think will make it stop?"

Lang glared at Mai. "Someday, the soldiers will be gone. Someday, people won't hate us because we are Hoa. Someday, even women will play on football teams in Vietnam, just like men."

"Someday may be a long way off," Mai said.

Their father came from behind the pharmacy counter where he finished filling the meager prescriptions they still got. It was time for practice and lately, Ba walked Lang there alone because Mai was still too angry to go with them.

"Ba, many of our Hoa friends have left Vietnam. Don't you think it's time for us to start a new life somewhere else?" Mai was annoyed when her father didn't say anything. Could he really believe they were safe? The few friends she still had were Hoa. They talked about vandalism and threats they received. Ba seemed to ignore the menacing soldiers and vandalism all around them while most of their friends planned their exit from Vietnam.

Ba motioned for Lang, who brushed past Mai, intentionally knocking her aside. She grabbed her duffel bag and walked out the door. Without saying another word, Ba followed. Mai groaned in frustration.

Ba usually returned after dropping Lang off, and while he was gone, Mai decided to work on the store's inventory. She was proud that her father trusted her to reorder supplies. Ma had a heart condition that often left her tired, and her father wasn't in the store as much as he used to be so he could help at home. She walked around the store, noting products they were running out of. With money tight and hardly anybody coming into the store, Mai needed to decide which products they should still stock.

As she worked, animated voices came from outside and Mai strained to listen. She was sure one voice belonged to Giang, an old friend from school. It would be nice to talk to friends, and Giang was always so funny and kind. The voices outside the store grew louder with laughter. Mai hopped down from her stool, ready to leave her work and join the fun. She slipped on a light jacket and stepped outside.

Three soldiers stood in front of the pharmacy. She was mistaken. Giang wasn't part of the group. As she watched them, a patch of gray clouds skittered across the sky until they covered the sun. The day suddenly got dark and gloomy. Mai turned to walk back into the store. She didn't notice a tall soldier with dark hair sweeping across his forehead, until he grabbed her arm and pulled her close to the wall. "Let go. Leave me alone," she demanded.

Mai struggled to get free, pulling his hand off her and then chomping down on it with all her might. The soldier yelled out. She turned to run, but the soldier grabbed her by the shoulders and spun her around toward the grimy brick wall beside the store window. Then he shoved her hard. Mai caught herself from falling by reaching out to touch the wall. Strange. Her hands felt wet and sticky and were covered in swirls of red and black paint. Confused, Mai looked up. A threat was spray-painted in huge letters that covered most of the wall.

GO BACK TO CHINA HOA

Mai gasped, bringing her hand to her mouth, and the paint covering her hands smeared across her face. She imagined herself looking like a cartoon clown. The soldiers laughed. Mai turned toward the soldiers, searching for a way to escape. Someone shoved her hard, and her head slammed against the wall. Mai wasn't sure if it was the growing lump on the back of her head or fear that made her dizzy. The sticky paint burned her face and her skin prickled.

From far away, she heard a voice. "Leave her alone. Get back to your posts." Mai looked up to see another soldier appear. He put his arm around her and propelled her back into the pharmacy.

The soldier helped her to a stool. "Are you okay?"

She nodded, too frightened to talk. He turned to leave. "Be careful outside. My comrades do not like the Hoa. I won't be able to protect you next time."

Ba returned just as the soldier left. Between sobs, she told him what happened. He went to a sink behind the counter to wet a washcloth. She shuddered, stunned that anyone could be so cruel, as he gently wiped her face and hands. They sat next to each other for a long time, Mai softly crying while leaning against her father. The sun began to set and the dim yellow lights inside the store flickered. Through the window, they watched people walk by, stopping to read the ugly message on the wall that glowed in the streetlights.

Mai and Ba jumped when Lang burst through the front door, breathing heavy with rage. "You forgot to pick me up. I waited there for a half hour and then walked home. Ba, who wrote that awful message?"

Ba blinked. "I'm sorry. Something happened."

A red flush crept up Lang's cheeks. "What?"

Mai recounted every detail, beginning with her delight when she thought friends were waiting for her outside and ending when the soldier helped her back inside. She hung her head. "It was awful. I'm so scared of what will happen next."

Ba nodded. His voice shook and his lips quivered. "If that soldier hadn't shown up, Mai would have been seriously injured or worse. This changes things. I can no longer protect my family." Ba placed one hand over the other to stop them from shaking. "We need to leave Vietnam."

Lang shook her head. "Things will get better here. I know they will."

"It's only gotten worse," Mai said. "Ba, where will we go?"

Ba touched a finger to his chin. "I never considered leaving, but I've listened to my friends talking. The United States offers the most opportunity. Mai, you could open a store. Lang, they have football teams for girls there. In a few years, you could play for an American college."

Lang was quiet, and Mai wondered if she was thinking about playing football in college, something that women in Vietnam couldn't do. She grabbed Lang's hand. "This might be the start of a better life."

9 ~ A Terrible Ending
2024

When Kim got out of the car, Charlotte and Mason were leaning against the fence at the entrance to the field. She shot them a grateful look. "Hey, thanks for coming."

"I don't know anybody who's worked harder this season. Kim, you've got this," Mason said and gave her a high five. Kim's stomach stopped its nervous tumble and she already felt better.

Charlotte wrapped her arms around Kim. "We're your cheering section today. We'll be watching from the bleachers. Go get 'em." Kim smiled. Seeing her team already starting to warm up, she waved goodbye to Charlotte and Mason and ran onto the field.

The team formed two lines with the person in one line kicking the ball to a person in the other line, who kicked the ball into the goal. Kim fell in line behind Stella, a tall blonde-haired girl who had the best passing skills on the team. "Hey," Stella said, grinning at Kim. "I'm so psyched. I think we're gonna go all the way this year."

Stella was always so positive that it made Kim feel better just being around her. Before she could respond, all the girls around her fell out of line and started talking at once. Their excitement was contagious. Someone else piped in, "We're going to own the field today."

Kim saw the shadow of a person standing right behind her. "That's if Kim doesn't mess it up again." Without turning her head, she knew it was Jayna. First Aunt Lang and now Jayna. Double whammy. Before she could respond, the coach blew his whistle, and the girls got back in line. Kim willed herself to focus on the game.

When she got to the front of the line, Kim executed a perfect kick. The person in the other line met the ball and kicked it cleanly in the goal. Kim shot a satisfied smirk as she glanced at Jayna, who scowled and looked away. Coach blew his whistle again and the team jogged to the sideline, ready to start the game.

* * *

They won! Kim's team gathered at the edge of the soccer field. They each placed an arm in the center of the circle, hand on top of hands, and cheered. Kim felt especially proud since she passed the ball to Stella who scored the winning goal. Charlotte and Mason cheered for Kim from the sidelines.

As the team celebrated their victory, Kim noticed Jayna whispering in the ears of several teammates. They nodded. When Jayna whispered in Stella's ear, Stella looked down, briefly glancing at Kim, before averting her eyes. Not even that dampened Kim's spirits. She left the cluster of celebrating girls and jogged over to her two best friends.

"See, I said you would come back better than ever," Charlotte squealed.

Mason playfully punched her in the arm. "Do you think your aunt will let you walk to Dooley's for ice cream?"

"I was thinking my team might go out for pizza, but most of them said they are busy, so I'd love to go to Dooley's. I'll call Aunt Lang and ask." Kim changed out of her cleats, shoved them into her duffel bag, and hoisted it to her shoulder. They headed toward the parking lot, cell phones in hand. "I'm not looking forward to talking to her."

Mason glanced at her. "Kim, why do you think your aunt is so mean to you?"

She thought about Aunt Lang and her disinterest, no....hatred of soccer. When Kim was younger, Lang didn't seem as moody. Kim remembered bursting into a room after finding some treasure outside, and Lang would smile. When she was three or four, Aunt Lang sang lullabies to her when she was sick. Unlike Grandma Mai, who sang melodic lullabies in Vietnamese, Lang's lullabies were American. To others, Lang was as cranky as a barnyard cat with an empty milk bowl. Everyone thought of Lang as disagreeable and mean, except Kim.

All that changed when Kim discovered soccer when she was five. As she spent more and more time chasing a soccer ball around the back yard or kicking goals with her dad, Lang retreated into her sullen shell. Even Kim couldn't get her to smile anymore. In fact, it seemed that she was the one who made Lang even grumpier. One time, Kim asked Aunt Lang why she was so crabby. Lang mumbled something about rude little girls, her parents reprimanded her for irritating Lang, and she vowed never to ask again.

"Earth to Kim," Mason said after her silence. "Are you still with us?"

Kim broke out of her thoughts. "Sorry. I'm not sure why Aunt Lang acts the way she does. It's weird, and my family doesn't talk about it, but nothing is going to spoil this day." She quickly made her call to Aunt Lang. The three friends talked and laughed as they walked.

Opening the door to Dooley's, Charlotte stepped in first and came to a sudden stop. Kim and Mason tried to get around her, but she didn't move. Laughter, and the sweet smell of ice cream and cookies drifted from the shop. Kim gave Charlotte a playful shove and they all entered the shop. She stared at a table in the corner, laughter spilling out from it and filling the room. Her team was gathered around the table, celebrating. Without her. Kim's stomach clenched when she saw Stella stop laughing and look away.

Kim wanted to walk over to the table and say some clever, cutting remark, but she was too stunned to think of one. It was just like her to never come up with the right thing to say at the right moment. Absent a clever comeback, Kim wanted to run out of the store and just go home. No. That would give Jayna too much satisfaction. Meeting up at Dooleys must have been what she was whispering to her teammates after the game.

Instead Kim braced herself and walked straight to the counter. Charlotte and Mason trailed behind her. "I'll take a scoop of Superman and a scoop of chocolate."

The team returned to their chatter, but Kim knew they were watching her. She looked over at their table, gave a quick wave, and then grabbed her cone. After Charlotte and Mason got their cones, they went outside and sat at a table outside the store. Kim could almost feel Jayna's eyes burning into her back when she walked out.

Mason elbowed Kim. "That was awesome. I can't believe you waved at Jayna. Talk about not giving her the satisfaction she wanted. That was the perfect response."

"Are you okay? I know it was hard, but you handled that so well," Charlotte said. Where Mason took on that "fight back" attitude, Kim knew Charlotte felt her pain.

Kim nodded. "Ever since you suggested it, Mason, I've been thinking about telling Coach Tim, but I know Jayna. She'll just find ways to bully me when he isn't around. It won't help."

Charlotte moved her chair closer to Kim and grinned. "Let's forget about Jayna for now. We're here to celebrate." The three of them raised their cones in a cheer, but the mood remained somber. After finishing their ice cream, Kim hugged Charlotte and Mason. "Thanks for being there for the game and for me." Heaving her bag over her shoulder, she started walking toward home.

from the [illegible] Kim ca[illegible] [illegible] playful sho[illegible] and [illegible]. [illegible]ed the shoe. She stared at [illegible] in their faces, laughter [illegible] out from [illegible] filling the room. Her team was gathered around the table, [illegible] when she saw the [illegible] laughing and [illegible] look away.

[illegible] to walk over to the table and say something, [illegible] [illegible] to think of one. It was [illegible] [illegible] [illegible] [illegible] right [illegible] say all the right [illegible]. [illegible] [illegible] Kim [illegible] to [illegible] of the shoe [illegible] [illegible] would give [illegible] [illegible] [illegible] must have been what she was whispering to her teammates [illegible] the [illegible].

[illegible] Kim [illegible] and walked [illegible] to the [illegible] [illegible] and Mas[illegible] [illegible] [illegible] like a scoop of Superman [illegible]

[illegible]

10 ~The Grand Plan 1977

All week, Mai watched Ba wrestle with the decision to leave Vietnam. Even after the frightening incident with the soldiers outside the pharmacy, he still questioned if they should leave. Once, she heard him on the phone, talking to his cousin.

"I don't want to go, but I'm worried about Mai and Lang's safety. I want to be sure it is the right decision."

Mai knew her family was one of thousands that was forced to make the same choice.

Later, Mai, Lang, and their parents sat around a pretty wicker table outside their apartment. Once the decision was made, the Kiens plunged into planning. In less than a month, they would be gone. They spoke in nervous bursts. Ba and Ma worried about adjusting to life in a new country, but Lang was swept up in the excitement of playing high school and college football. "It will be hard to leave, but I'm ready. I've heard women can play professional football in the United States and even kids play in big tournaments. They call it soccer."

Mai hoped they would end up in San Francisco or another city along the ocean, but they wouldn't know exactly where they would live until they arrived. A sponsor, usually a church or volunteer group, would find them a home and help them get settled.

"I heard that San Francisco is a wondrous place with tall buildings and a wharf filled with seafood," Ma said. Then she grew quiet. "I'll miss Vietnam. Nowhere else will you find the beautiful white frangipani flowers or the bright red flame trees. Mostly, I'll miss my cousins." Ma's fingers touched the gold necklace that reached mid-chest as she talked.

Ba wrapped his arm around Ma. "There will be many opportunities for all of us in the United States. We'll help Mai open the store she is dreaming of. As soon as we arrive, I'll search for the best school and soccer team for Lang." He smiled at Lang.

The family reviewed their plans. The government stopped flights out of Vietnam when the war ended, so they would be taking a two day bus ride to Hong Kong and flying to the United States from there. While they talked, they snacked on sugar cane shrimp and Pho rolls, and sipped rice wine. Excitement coursed through Mai like electricity surging through wire. She was young and ambitious. Moving to a new country would be the start of her dream to own a store that would sell fun home decor.

Ba smiled at his family. "Let's toast to our future." Lang, Mai and Ba raised their glasses. Ma sighed and raised her glass too. Mai felt proud of her father for stepping up to protect his family. She was confident this was the beginning of a better life.

11 ~ The Quitter
2024

The day after the winning playoff game and the Dooley's ice cream disaster, Kim reluctantly showed up for practice. She didn't want to go, but the next game was Saturday, and she wanted to start in it. Arriving a little late so she didn't have to talk to anyone before practice, Kim watched the rest of the team kick their soccer balls between tall yellow cones. They looked like daffodils sprouting from the green grass.

She spotted Jayna swiftly moving from side to side, expertly maneuvering the ball between the cones. Kim grabbed her ball from the basket where everyone stored them between practices. "Soft," she muttered as she squeezed the ball between her hands, deflating it even more. She looked around for the pump, but it wasn't in its usual spot next to the basket.

"Kim, you're late," Coach yelled from across the field. "Get a move on it."

Noticing there weren't any other balls, Kim dropped the slightly deflated one on the ground and gave it a hard kick. It landed with a thump five feet in front of her. Jayna snickered while watching Kim attempt to dribble the ball onto the field. The rest of her teammates looked away. She wondered if they felt embarrassed to be part of the joke or if they were trying not to laugh in front of the coach.

"It seems my ball lost air," Kim said to her coach, not bothering to hide her sarcasm. "I wonder how that happened." She followed up with an eye roll and looked pointedly at Jayna. Coach Tim glanced at Jayna; his eyes boring into her. Then he kicked the ball under his foot to Kim. Grateful, she caught it and left the deflated ball laying at the edge of the field. Jayna glared at her and Kim looked away, pretending she didn't see. When she joined the rest of the team, Jayna bumped her and mumbled, "Go away, Gook. We don't want you here."

Kim blinked and her jaw dropped. Gook? She only heard that word one other time. It was a mean, ugly word. A word people in the United States called the Vietnamese during the war. She heard it in a movie and asked her dad what it meant. He sounded angry when he explained. Kim knew she was part Vietnamese, but why would Jayna call her that?

For the rest of practice, Jayna cut Kim off, roughly pushed her out of the way, and bullied the rest of the team into not passing the ball to her. It got so bad that even Coach Tim noticed and blew his whistle. "Jayna, that would've been a perfect time to pass to Kim. Keep an eye on who's closest to you."

Kim was annoyed that Coach Tim didn't realize it was intentional. One time, she tried to pass the ball to a teammate, but they all looked away. "Kim, that's a Holding penalty. Pass the ball when you get it," Coach said. Throughout the practice, he constantly yelled orders to her. "Stay on your feet. Follow the ball. Go after that ball. Be a team player."

Finally, Kim lost her patience. "I AM a team player. Leave me alone!" She kicked the soccer ball as hard as she could across the field. It whizzed by Coach Tim's head and hit the fence.

His mouth set in a firm line. "Poor sportsmanship has no place on this team," Coach shouted, stalking toward her. "Until your attitude changes, you're on the bench."

Fuming, Kim retrieved the ball and stalked off the field. She plopped down on a bench and made herself take deep, calming breaths. Kim remained on the bench until practice was over and all the girls were gone. She watched her coach pack up, handing him the clipboard and first aid kit that were still laying on the bench. "Coach, I'm sorry."

He sat down next to her. "This isn't like you, Kim. I thought you were going to be my top player this year, but lately, your inability to work with the team is getting in the way. What's going on?"

Kim couldn't believe that Coach was blaming her. This wasn't going to be easy. She decided to plunge ahead. "It's Jayna. She doesn't like me, and she's turned the whole team against me."

Coach Tim exhaled loudly. "I noticed tension between you and Jayna and thought you might be having friendship issues. Is that what this was about today? I'll talk to Jayna."

Kim gulped. Would he just make the problem worse? Probably. She hesitated, regretting she brought it up. Jayna wasn't going to magically stop the bullying because Coach asked her to. She would just be sneakier. Or just bully her off the soccer field. "No, don't. I think this is something Jayna and I need to figure out."

He sat for a moment before looking at his watch. "I have a coaches' meeting in twenty minutes. You and Jayna need to work this out before Saturday. Let me know if you want my help."

So much for talking to the coach, Kim thought as she watched him pick up the bag of balls and walk off the field. It wasn't like Jayna would open up to the coach and explain why she was being a bully. Kim knew it was up to her to figure out Jayna. With a pit in her stomach and a broken heart, Kim saw Aunt Lang's car facing the soccer field, and headed toward it.

"Why did you kick that ball at your coach?" Lang asked Kim after she settled in the passenger side of the car and slammed the door. "You need to apologize."

How long had Aunt Lang been watching? She never seemed interested in anything Kim did before. "I did, but it doesn't matter," Kim said through clenched teeth, "because I quit."

Lang glared. "So you're a quitter as well as a bad soccer player?"

Kim sat statue still, staring ahead. Of course, Aunt Lang wouldn't understand. Lang sat up straighter and blew air out of slightly open lips. "Are you going to let that girl get the best of you?" Lang's voice was soft, almost caring.

Kim was stunned. Her aunt, who hated soccer and never showed any interest in it, noticed Jayna's antics. Other parents didn't notice. Even Coach Tim didn't notice how bad it was. Surprised, Kim realized that Aunt Lang must have watched the entire practice from her car. Kim scrunched down in the passenger side of the car and glared at Aunt Lang. "What do you care? You don't understand soccer or what it's like to be hated because of who you are."

"You don't know what real hate is," Lang whispered. The two sat in angry silence for a long time and Kim noticed Lang's eyes blinking, like she was trying not to cry.

"Why is that girl bullying you?"

Lang was going back and forth between caring and mean. Confused, Kim looked at her. "Her name is Jayna, and every day at practice she torments me. She lets the air out of my ball and shoves me out of the way when I go for a pass. Today, she called me a gook."

Lang gasped. She reached out and placed her thin, brown hand on Kim's shoulder. "Sometimes it is hard to be different and people use those differences as an excuse to be mean. Is being Vietnamese really Jayna's reason for bothering you or could there be something else?"

"I don't know," Kim said. "I just want her to stop so I can focus on playing soccer." Although she was frustrated and sad, Kim was also amazed Aunt Lang was comforting her. Lang believed you should be tough. She wasn't one to coddle or show her feelings. Kim's spirits brightened as the two sat in the car talking about Jayna.

"Aunt Lang, lately, I haven't been able to do anything right on the soccer field. My mind is always on Jayna and what she'll do next. Mason and Charlotte think she's jealous, but I know it's more than that. She hates me." The words tumbled out of Kim's mouth like a fast moving river current. "I'm good at soccer, really good. I think I could play in college and be in the Olympics one day."

Lang suddenly withdrew her arm from around Kim. Her lips pursed together as if she just sucked on a lemon. "You aren't that good." With that, the magical spell was broken. Kim curled up on the seat and stared out the window as the car rolled out of the parking lot.

12 The Right Decision? 1977

Two weeks after Mai's family sat around the table celebrating their decision to move, disaster changed their plans. Mai was visiting a friend when she heard the news. The Hong Kong and Thai governments were overwhelmed by the number of Vietnamese entering their countries and threatened to close their borders. Watching the newscast on TV, worry sat like a rock on her chest.

"My family can't stay in Vietnam, but soon, there won't be any place to go," Mai fretted. She heard other countries would limit the number of refugees crossing their border within the next few weeks.

Mai's friend seemed confident. "My family is staying here. With pressure from other countries, we think our government will change how they treat us. I've heard people talk about how dangerous it is to leave, and it scares me."

"The only danger is if you escape illegally on one of those fishing boats. My family can afford to travel by bus and plane," Mai said, but there was a nervous edge to her voice. "We just need to leave before Hong Kong and Thailand close their borders." Soon after, Mai said a final goodbye to her friend and went home.

She found her parents huddled at the wicker table in the garden, quietly talking. "Ba and Ma, on the news it said Vietnam is under pressure to stop people from leaving. If we wait any longer, we might not be able to leave."

Her parents weren't nodding in agreement and seemed hesitant to talk. Something was wrong. "Did you hear me, Ba? We need to leave. Soon."

Finally, her father seemed to find his words. "Mai, you are brave, ambitious, and hopeful. You will have much success in America, but Ma and I think the journey to the United States will be difficult now. Your mother's heart isn't strong. With all the new restrictions in place, travel will be hard—"

Mai's stomach clenched. She knew what her parents were about to say and didn't want to hear it. "It will be hard," she said, cutting her father off. "But I'll be there to help you and Ma. Please. We are a family and must leave together."

Ba shook his head. Ma looked down. "Mai," her father began again, his voice firm. "You and Lang must go to America, but your mother and I will stay here and move in with my cousin."

"I can't leave you." Mai's voice was thin and scared. "I'm only seventeen. How will I take care of myself, let alone Lang?"

He stood up and hugged Mai. "I've made my decision. You and Lang will leave together, and your sponsor will help you get settled in the United States. Ma and I can come later when the airports open again." He avoided looking at Mai, his head turned down, and trudged into the house.

Ma gave Mai a sad, crooked smile. "It breaks my heart, but it's the only way you will have a good life. You must go. We'll be fine." She rose and stood across from Mai. Her soft, dark hair was pulled into a bun that perched at the top of her graceful neck. Mai looked at Ma's beautiful golden heart necklace glimmering against her chest. The heart curled at the tip into a tiny circle. When she was little, Mai often cradled the heart in her hand as Ma explained the circle slipping from the end of the heart symbolized family circling around each other in support.

Ma bent her head and removed the sparkling necklace from around her neck. She gently placed the necklace around Mai's neck and fastened the clasp. Ma always called it the *lòng can đảm* necklace — the Courage necklace. "Many years ago, your great grandma gave this necklace to your grandma before she immigrated from China to Vietnam. She said it would bring her courage when things got tough or scary. Now, you'll wear the necklace to give you courage."

Mai knew she wouldn't convince her parents to come. "No, I can't take your necklace." Panic at the thought of traveling alone with Lang made her heart beat faster and her face burn.

Ma placed her hand over the heart. "You can give it back to me when the airports open and we join you." Those words gave Mai hope. The heart now rested in the center of her chest, and a sense of calm and courage replaced the panic.

13 ~ Not My Business 2024

When they got to Aunt Lang's house, Kim kicked her shoes off and went upstairs. She slammed the door and dropped onto her bed. She must have dozed off because she woke to the phone ringing loudly. She listened to a muted conversation between Lang and someone. She tried to make out the conversation.

"... Is the pharmacy still there?"

"... How is Mai holding up?"

"... Did she visit Ba and Ma's grave?"

Through the window, Kim saw the sunset leaving purple and pink streaks across the darkening sky. That meant it was morning in Vietnam and Lang was talking to her parents. Kim hadn't talked to them since they left because of the time difference, but she did get a text message, telling her they arrived safely and asking about the playoff game.

Lang barged into Kim's room, phone in hand. "Kim, it's your mom."

Kim tentatively took the phone—afraid something was wrong with Grandma Mai. "Hi, Mom. Is everything okay?"

Her mom's voice sounded far away and staticky. "Yes. Vietnam is such a beautiful country. Grandma is enjoying seeing her cousins."

Kim felt the tense muscles in her shoulders relax. "Oh. It sounded like Aunt Lang was worried about Grandma."

"Grandma has good and bad memories of Vietnam, and sometimes it makes her sad. Most of the time, she is happy."

Then Mom switched topics to soccer. Kim didn't have the heart to tell her things weren't going well with soccer or Lang. She forced herself to sound cheerful. "Everything's fine. We won our first playoff game, and Aunt Lang and I are having a great time."

Aunt Lang's lips turned up into a slight smile and she rolled her eyes. Kim looked away, pretending not to see. Her mom must have noticed the edge in her voice. "Are you sure? Is Lang treating you well and taking you to practices?"

"It's all good," Kim said, "but I miss you." The static on the line grew louder so Kim said goodbye.

Taking the phone back, Aunt Lang was quiet. Kim realized she knew very little about Grandma Mai and Lang's early lives. It must have been hard to leave your family and move to a new country, but there had to be more to it. "Aunt Lang, why would Grandma have bad memories?"

Lang turned her back and walked out of the room. As she left, Kim could hear her grumble. "It is none of your business. Leave well enough alone."

"Why is everything that happens in this family not my business?" Kim shouted at the door. Aunt Lang didn't bother to answer. Something tragic happened in Vietnam forty-six years ago. It explained why Aunt Lang and Grandma never talked about life in Vietnam. Their early life was a mystery, and Kim was determined to figure it out.

14 ~ Time to Leave 1977

Mai rushed into the room, a suitcase in one hand and clothes in the other. She set them down and arranged the clothes in neat piles. Lang blew into the house like she was riding the wind. She dropped her backpack before yelling, "Mai, where are you? I have great news."

Mai looked up. "Right here. We need to talk."

Lang held up her ribbon. "We won our game." She danced around the living room, the ribbon fluttering in her fingers. "I wasn't even bothered when everyone ignored me."

Mai's throat tightened when Ba and Ma quietly slipped into the room. Lang stopped dancing. "What's wrong? Why are you packing a suitcase? We aren't leaving for two more weeks," Lang said, her voice rising with each question.

Ba sat on the old floral couch and motioned for Lang to sit next to him. "Countries are closing their doors to us, but the bus stations are still open. Lang, you need to leave tomorrow, or you may never get out."

Lang stood still. "You? What do you mean? Don't you mean 'we'?"

Ba's face crinkled, but his voice was firm. "Your mother's heart isn't strong enough for the kind of trip you'll need to take. You and Mai will leave tomorrow and we'll join you when the airports reopen."

Lang frowned. "Without you and Ma, I won't go. Can't we leave with you when the airports reopen?"

Mai was honest with Lang. "It could be months or longer, and travel will become more dangerous before it gets better. This is our opportunity to leave, to get to the United States."

Lang faced Ba, listing reasons why she should stay in Vietnam. Ba countered each argument. "Oh, Ba. I want to move to the United States, but I can't imagine going without you and Ma."

Ba seemed to be waffling on his decision. "Maybe …" His voice was drowned out by a loud bang echoing through the apartment. The front window shook, and glass crackled as it broke into a thousand tiny pieces. A large gray rock flew through the window and over the couch where they were sitting. It landed in the middle of the living room and rolled against the leg of a chair. Glass sprinkled down on them in sparkling diamond-shaped pieces.

Mai turned and looked out the window. A soldier stood below, laughing. Ba picked up the rock and looked out, too. He dropped it as if it were a hot coal. Small shards of glass glistened in his hair. Lang had several spots of blood on her hands. Mai felt drops of blood clustering near the corner of her mouth.

Ba paced across the room and then turned toward Lang. "You and Mai will leave tomorrow. I will not have my daughters harmed. This is not open for discussion."

Staying in Vietnam scared Mai. "I'm leaving tomorrow and don't want to go alone. Lang, please come with me."

15 ~ That's What Friends Are For 2024

The next morning, Kim woke, restless, and sad. How could she possibly get through two more weeks without her parents? Whenever she had a problem with school, friends, or anything else, she could count on them to listen and problem-solve. Without her mom bringing in that basket of laundry to fold, she never felt more alone.

The day was overcast and cool, which matched Kim's mood perfectly. Thankfully, it was the team's rest day, so she could put off dealing with Jayna and Coach Tim for one more day. While she was getting dressed, her phone chimed. Glancing at the text, Kim smiled.

It was Charlotte. *Can u hang out at the mall 2day? My mom can drive.*

Suddenly, the day seemed less gloomy. They would shop, eat at the food court, and maybe catch a movie at the mall theater. Then Kim frowned. Would Aunt Lang actually let her go to the mall after the fiasco with kicking the ball and storming off the field yesterday? Lang was big on respecting adults, even if Kim believed she was justified. She'd have to come up with a good reason why she should be allowed to go.

Kim's thumbs tapped her phone. *Yeah, but gotta ask Lang.*

Then she headed downstairs, listening to Aunt Lang unloading the dishwasher. Might as well ask now so she could let Charlotte know. She grabbed an apple from the fridge and ate it with one hand while putting away the silverware from the dishwasher with the other. Being helpful when you want something never hurt.

Lang glanced at Kim, raising her eyebrows, but didn't say anything. Kim never helped with chores when she visited. "Yesterday was a rough day for me. I really miss Mom and Dad." Lang's shoulders relaxed and she seemed to soften. "I was hoping to take my mind off things by spending the day with Charlotte. She invited me to the mall." Kim took the plates from Aunt Lang's hands and put them away. "Do you think I could go?" She slumped her shoulder and shot her aunt the "puppy dog" look.

"Hmpphhh." Lang took a deep breath and seemed to be considering her answer. "Who would take you? I don't have time to drive you to soccer *and* the mall. I have things I need to get done."

Kim's spirits rose. "We don't have practice today and Charlotte said her mom could drive. Then you can take the whole day to get your work done." She didn't bring up quitting. It wasn't the right time.

"Okay," Lang said after hesitating for a moment. "But be back in time for dinner."

It worked! Kim squealed and grabbed her phone to text Charlotte. An hour later, they were on their way to the mall.

Charlotte and Kim spent the morning going to their favorite stores. A new shirt and leggings certainly brightened the day. Next, they headed to the food court where Charlotte got a slice of pizza and Kim grabbed a burger. They met at a table near the perimeter.

Charlotte lifted the gooey slice of pizza and used her fingers to break the stringy cheese apart. "You seemed kind of quiet this morning. Something wrong?"

"It's Jayna. Again." Kim rehashed everything that happened at practice yesterday, including Jayna calling her a gook and her talking to the coach. With her parents not being around, it felt really good to have someone to talk to.

"What's a gook?" Charlotte asked.

"It's a nasty name for an Asian person. It's weird that Jayna even knows that word. Nobody uses it anymore."

Charlotte shrugged. "What are you going to do?"

"I'll tell Mom and Dad when they come back. I'm sure they'll have some suggestions," Kim said. "Until then, I just don't know. I've thought about quitting."

Charlotte opened her mouth to speak, but suddenly closed it. She pointed behind Kim. Turning in her chair, Kim spotted Jayna and two friends in line at the taco counter. "I can't believe it," she said. "I just can't escape her." The happy mood of the day was replaced by despair.

"Don't look now," Charlotte said, "but they're heading toward us." They hung their heads and ate in silence, hoping Jayna didn't notice them. Kim spotted movement out of the corner of her eye. She looked up and saw Jayna and her followers perched right beside them, like squirrels waiting for a nut.

"Hi, Charlotte. Hi, Kim. I didn't know you were going to be here today," Jayna chirped, her voice rising. "Do you mind if we sit here?"

Dumbfounded, Kim couldn't find her voice for a moment. Strange. Jayna was actually being friendly. Maybe she felt bad about yesterday's soccer practice? Kim's thoughts wavered between disbelief and hope.

Shooting Charlotte a confused look, she shrugged her shoulders. "Sure."

Charlotte mouthed, "No," but it was too late. The three girls pulled up chairs from a nearby table and spread their food out. Conversation flowed as they quickly changed topics from the new clothing store to the cute guy working at American Eagle, to the best movie playing at the theater. Kim was relieved that nobody brought up the topic of soccer. Charlotte remained uncharacteristically quiet, but Kim relaxed and began to enjoy the lunch.

When only wadded-up food wrappers were left on the table, Jayna gathered her drink and wrappers on her tray and stood. Her friends followed, like minions on a movie screen. "Well, this was fun," Jayna said, smiling widely. "We're off to the arcade." In an exaggerated movement, Jayna slipped her foot under the leg of Kim's chair. She tumbled forward, using the table to regain her balance, but not before her tray upended and clattered to the ground.

Dirty wrappers rained down around Kim. A nearly full soda landed on her lap, the plastic lid popped open, and cold soda ran down her legs like an icy river. Kim jumped up, sending the wrappers skittering across the floor, and shook off the rivulets of soda trickling down her leg. "Oh my God. What did you do?"

Jayna smirked. Her friends backed away, distancing themselves from Kim and maybe even Jayna. "I'm so sorry. It really was an accident." But Jayna's voice didn't match her words. They were syrupy sweet with a hint of laughter. "I sure hope you can get cleaned up and still make that movie." She tossed her mane of blonde hair back and motioned for her friends, who followed her like puppies drawn to their mother.

After Jayna walked away, laughing, Kim stood there, soda dripping from her. Charlotte ran to a counter, returned with a wad of napkins, and began blotting at Kim's shorts. A worker came over with a yellow bucket and mop and began sopping up the mess around her feet. Through it all, Kim didn't move.

Charlotte grabbed Kim's hand. "Come on, Kim. Let's go to the restroom and you can change into your new leggings. Going to the movie will take your mind off Jayna."

Kim dug her feet into the floor, resisting Charlotte's pull. "How could I be so stupid. I should have seen this coming."

Charlotte squeezed Kim's hands, and Kim could feel her warmth and kindness. "Kim, you didn't see this coming because you don't see the bad in people. Let's go to the movies. You can't let Jayna live rent free in your head."

Kim nodded. "Thanks for trying to make me feel better, Charlotte, but I think I want to go home. Can you call your mom?" Charlotte took off her jacket and wrapped it around Kim's waist. Then she called her mom. Picking up her bag, now sticky with soda, Kim followed Charlotte out of the mall. How could a day that started out so well turn into such a disaster?

16 ~ Final Goodbye 1977

The morning after the rock tore through the Kien's window, Lang and Mai walked out the front door of the pharmacy, overstuffed backpacks hanging from their shoulders. Ma and Ba followed. The evening before was bittersweet, filled with serious conversation, but also laughter as Ba entertained them with stories about when they were little.

Now, standing outside, Mai felt like she turned into an adult overnight. How could she be excited and frightened at the same time? She raised her chin, trying to appear calm and brave. "Don't worry. We'll write as soon as we arrive in the United States. How long do you think it will be before you and Ma join us?"

Ba's frowned. "It's hard to tell. It will be a while for the communist government to finish making changes." He didn't sound confident, and Mai avoided asking for details that might upset Lang.

Ma adjusted Lang's backpack and Ba placed his hands on her shoulders. "Lang, work hard in school and on the football field. Make us proud. When we arrive, the first thing Ma and I want to do is watch your games. Imagine, in just a few short years, my daughter will be playing football for an American college." His smile reflected pride.

Lang's mouth quivered. "What will Mai and I do without you?"

Ba pulled her close. "In Vietnam, it is a father's job to take care of his daughters, but the war changed how I can do that. I raised both of you to be strong, independent women. With all my heart, I believe you will have much success in America, but you must go now."

Lang looked up at Ba and smiled. "I'll work hard and make you proud. I expect to see you waving at me from the stands when I'm playing for the U.S. Women's National Team someday."

Before walking out to the waiting taxi, they gave their parents a fierce hug and then turned away. Mai was glad Ma and Ba walked back into the store before they got in the taxi and headed across town to the bus station. Watching them as the taxi pulled away would hurt too much.

Mai's stomach flip-flopped with sadness, intense excitement, and trepidation. It seemed foolish for two young girls to travel alone to another country. How would they manage the long trip and living in a new country by themselves? Worry coursed through Mai like a raging river, but she didn't want it to show. Before getting in the taxi, she looked at Lang and grinned. "Our new life is just beginning."

Lang slid in the taxi and Mai scooted in next to her. Lang smiled. "I keep telling myself that, soon, I'll be playing football in the United States."

Mai nodded. "I believe you will." Then she turned toward the window and looked at the aging buildings and busy streets, trying to absorb the sights and sounds before they disappeared. They passed Vinhomes Park, where Lang played, and her old school. It was hard to believe that she may never see those places again. Soon, the massive bus station appeared.

When they entered, Mai looked in dismay at the long lines ending at the ticket counter and winding like evil snakes from the entrance. Young adults clutching backpacks, elderly men struggling with massive suitcases, tired families with crying children, and bewildered couples clutching each other's hands were jammed together. Shouts filled the air as those at the front of the line fought to buy tickets to anywhere. Mai froze in place, frightened by the shouting and thousands of people surrounding them. Pushed along by people trying to enter the bus station, they moved through the throng of people. A sharp elbow jabbed into Mai's side and she yelped in surprise.

A short man in a dark green jacket and pressed brown pants jostled against Mai. "I am so sorry. Are you okay?"

Mai nodded. The noise made it difficult to talk, so Lang and Mai held hands and fought their way to the end of a line. The man followed behind and the line slowly inched forward. The air was hot and stagnant. It smelled of fear, sweat, and fried food. She glanced through the doorway behind her and saw a continual line of buses exiting the bus station. Overwhelmed, Mai's head pounded.

The man who accidentally elbowed Mai stared at her with big, kind eyes. He had a thick black mustache, and a white canvas hat perched on his head. "Where are you going?"

Mai was wary of strangers after her bad experiences on the streets near their home, but the man's smile seemed genuine. "Hong Kong first and then we'll take a plane to the United States. I'm Mai and this is my sister, Lang."

"I'm headed to Hong Kong too, and then Australia." He looked around. "Where are your parents?"

Lang looked so small against the crowd that enveloped them, but she exuded an aura of confidence as she spoke. "Ma isn't healthy enough to travel now. We are going to the United States, and they'll join us later."

The man nodded. "That is a wise decision. I work for the government and can see what is happening in Vietnam under Lê Duẩn's rule. I sent my family to Australia last year. Now, I'm heading there to meet them."

Mai felt better, knowing that other families were just like them. She wondered if they should have immigrated a year ago when fewer people were leaving. If it worked well for this man, then she believed things would work out for them too. The line moved forward a little, but the number of people entering the bus station seemed to swell before them. People bumped into each other, stepped on their toes, and rubbed sweaty arms.

They talked as they waited in line. The man looked at Mai and Lang. "You remind me of my own daughters, brave and independent. That will help you on your journey." Mai nodded and asked more about his daughters.

Time passed slowly and the line inched forward. Just as they were getting near the ticket booth, a voice boomed over the intercom. "All buses are full. Until further notice, the bus station is closed. Please leave immediately."

Mai panicked. Her plan to move to America already hit a snag. She turned to the man. "What should we do?"

"Since the communists are closing the bus station, I've heard escaping by ship from Vung Tau Beach on the South China Sea is safest," he said. "You can pay to board a ship sailing to Hong Kong or Indonesia. Go now." He pushed through the crowd, guiding Mai and Lang to the door of the bus station.

Mai pleaded with the man. "Please come with us. I'm scared."

He shook his head. "I've always had a terrible fear of water and don't think I could board a ship. I'll have to figure out another way." Before disappearing into the crowd, the man looked at them. "Trust me. Leaving Vietnam is the best thing, if you want a future."

Lang and Mai walked down the sidewalk to escape the crowd, their heavy backpacks hanging from their shoulders. Around the corner, it was cooler under an awning, the crowd was thinner, and a slight breeze blunted the noisiness of the bus station. They stood together, discussing their options. Mai wanted to take a taxi to Vung Tau where they could board a ship.

Lang was quiet for a moment and then offered a half-smile. "I think I trust that man at the bus station. He reminds me of Ba. Let's head to Vung Tau." Mai nodded. Before walking back to where taxis were lined up in front of the bus station, Mai heard a cry rise above the noise.

It alternated between a loud wail and a soft snuffle. They followed the puzzling sound to a narrow alley.

Mai stopped. "What is that?"

Lang looked around at the trash piled in the alley. "Let's go. We need to find a taxi."

Mai hesitated. "No, I think someone is hurt." They walked into the alley, following the sound to the back near a dumpster. Lang tossed the trash behind her as Mai leaned in and pulled out a teary-eyed, sniffling toddler.

17 ~ Hardship
2024

Kim and Charlotte didn't speak on the way home, wrapped in their own thoughts, and not wanting to get Charlotte's mom involved. Kim was sure Charlotte's mom noticed the pink jacket around her waist but was kind enough not to say anything. Charlotte helped her out of the car. "Get a shower. Then call me," she whispered before hugging Kim and getting back in the car.

Opening the front door, Kim slipped in. The door closed with a soft click, and she headed upstairs, trying to not alert Aunt Lang she was home until she had a chance to shower and put on clean clothes.

"Kim, you're home early," Lang called from the kitchen. "Good. You can help me cut up vegetables for dinner."

Darn. Lang must have supersonic ears. "Do you mind if I skip dinner? I'm not hungry after a big lunch and I'm really tired." Kim darted upstairs before Lang could answer. Stupid. Trusting. The butt of a good joke. That was how she felt. Kim usually tried to find the good in people, but what was she thinking? How could she believe that Jayna changed and wanted to be her friend? Was she that desperate? Twenty minutes later, Kim emerged from the bathroom with her hair wrapped in a towel. She grabbed a book and curled up under the covers.

The next morning, Kim stayed in bed, texting with Charlotte and Mason. They didn't know what to do about Jayna, but just texting with them made her feel better. Finally, Kim's grumbling stomach forced her to get up. Wandering downstairs, she found Lang in the kitchen, bent over the stove. She was stirring a pot of Chao Ga. Kim loved the bland rice porridge mixed with chicken. Ladling the porridge into a bowl for Kim, Lang said, "Practice is in forty-five minutes. Finish your Choa Ga and I will drive you."

Kim took the bowl and sat down at the table. "I'm not going." Her words came out as a thin whisper, and she wasn't even sure Aunt Lang heard her.

"Not going? So, you give up?" Lang said.

"Yes, I'm giving up. I'm tired of dealing with Jayna and her crew. It's not worth it."

Lang turned from the stove. "Maybe you shouldn't be avoiding her. Maybe you need to confront the problem, um, Jayna, instead of running away."

"Aunt Lang, you don't understand. It's not as simple as talking to Jayna." Lang listened while Kim complained about being bullied, soccer, and missing her parents.

Lang's cheeks grew red, and she slammed down the spoon she was using to stir the porridge. "You are the one who asked to stay behind when your parents wanted you to go, and now you are complaining. You don't know what hardship is." She took off her ruffled apron, and walked out of the room.

Kim opened her mouth, but no words came out. She followed Aunt Lang into the living room. "Aunt Lang, this *is* hard. I bet you were never bullied."

Lang spun around toward Kim. Her mouth was set in a thin pale line. She strode over to Kim and roughly grabbed her arm. "You will not quit. Get your bag and get in the car now."

Kim pulled her arm away from Aunt Lang, opened the front door, and ran out.

18 ~ A Tough Decision 1977

Mai lifted the toddler from behind the pile of trash while he flailed his arms, trying to push her away. A pair of dirty overalls and a light green cotton shirt hung on his thin body. His short black hair clung to his head in a dirty swirl. Based on his size, Mai guessed that he was three or four years old. After a few minutes, he stopped fighting and buried his head in Mai's chest. "Ma," he sniffed before his thumb found its way to his mouth.

Lang poked around behind the trash and pulled out a plastic bag containing a pair of socks, underwear, and a baggy holding cubes of bread. A tattered blue blanket was folded at the bottom of the bag. Lang dropped the bag. "A war orphan," she said.

Mai balanced the boy on her hip so she could see him better. "How old are you?" He lifted his head and held up three dirty fingers. Mai inhaled sharply. He was so young to be alone on the street. "What's your name, *đứa nhỏ?*" The boy was becoming more playful, twirling Mai's hair. Proudly, he looked her in the eye and said, "Tran."

Tran stared at Mai with eyes as blue and round as shiny marbles. His dirty face was streaked where tears made paths to his chin. "Oh," Mai gasped. "He's Amerasian. No wonder he was abandoned."

"We had a boy, like Tran, in my class whose dad was an American soldier," Lang said. When his dad was shipped back to the United States, he left his mom behind. Everyone taunted him. It's worse than being Hoa." Mai wrapped the old blue blanket around the little boy and held him close. Her heart hurt for him.

Lang popped a cube of bread into Tran's mouth, and he quickly swallowed it. She followed with another and Tran ate that just as fast. "I can't believe his mom would just leave him on the street."

Lang stared at Tran. "If we were staying in Vietnam, we could help him, but, Mai, we must get to Vung Tau Beach before dark. I've heard these kids learn to take care of themselves."

"We can't just leave him here," Mai pleaded. "He'll starve." She felt a connection to Tran. In Vietnam, Amerasians and the Hoa were both outcasts. "We can take him with us to the United States and find him a home." Mai stroked his hair and whispered to him.

Lang walked toward the front of the alley. "We can't take him with us. We're just kids ourselves. It would be impossible to take a toddler. Mai, be reasonable." At that moment, Mai felt like Lang was the grown-up and she was the little kid, begging to keep a stray puppy. Lang was usually the soft one.

Mai hesitated, squeezing Tran tightly to her. "He seems really smart and how much trouble can he be?"

Lang tried to pull Tran from Mai's grip, but he held on tighter, his heart beating loudly against her. "We need to leave Vietnam. We can't be slowed down by an Amerasian child. And we certainly don't have enough money to pay for his plane ticket," Lang said.

She sounded like a practical parent which made Mai sad that Lang was being forced to grow up quickly. Mai continued to stroke Tran's hair. He looked up and his lips curled into a shy smile. His grubby arms tightened around her neck, but she knew that taking a small child with them would make the trip difficult, if not impossible.

Lang tugged at Mai's elbow. "We need to leave. Now. The traffic is heavy and there aren't many cabs available." Mai nodded and tearfully sat Tran into the corner of the alley before tucking his soft blanket around him.

Tran looked up at Mai and his thin body trembled. His smile dropped and he stood up, grabbing at her pants and raising his arms to be held. She quickly headed out of the alley behind Lang, as Tran called after her and then crumpled into a heap, crying. Feeling sadness and regret, Mai looked back one last time. "Goodbye, Tran."

19 ~ Asking for Help 2024

Kim ran to the place she felt safest—her house. She looked around to make sure Aunt Lang hadn't followed and then punched in the garage code. Once inside, she climbed the steps two at a time and then curled up on her soft bed. It felt so good to be inside her own house, even if the air was warm and humid. The shade was closed, making the darkened room feel like her own cave.

Tapping the Messages icon on her phone, Kim thought about texting Charlotte and Mason to come over, but she didn't feel like talking to friends just yet. She thumbed through her phone, looking at Youtube videos instead. The tension oozed from her shoulders, and she began to relax.

A little surprised that Aunt Lang still hadn't come to find her, Kim raised the shade, expecting to see her, but the streets were empty except for a group of boys skateboarding. She glanced at the time on her phone. Practice started fifteen minutes ago and it felt strange, but a relief, not to be there.

Going downstairs, she took bottled water from the fridge and walked around the house, pondering when things started to go wrong between her and Jayna. When she first met Jayna four years ago, she thought they might become best friends. They were in third grade and Jayna was the new girl who just moved to Three Lakes. When her teacher asked who wanted to be a buddy to Jayna and show her around, Kim's hand shot up.

After their teacher chose her to be Jayna's buddy, they became close friends. On the third grade field trip to the zoo, Jayna and Kim were partners. They discovered they both had a talent for imitating animal sounds. Standing before each exhibit, mimicking the animals, had their classmates laughing so hard they were almost crying.

"I've been thinking about joining soccer," Jayna told Kim one day at the end of fourth grade. "Could you help me practice so I'll be good enough to be on your team?" Kim was excited and they met often at the park to practice. By the end of the summer, Jayna was ready.

During art class in fifth grade, Kim struggled with drawing the nose on her self-portrait. Frustrated, she put her pencil down and brushed the paper off the table. Jayna picked up the paper and sat beside Kim. "Let me help you. Your nose is too small which doesn't make it look real." Jayna drew a slightly rounded triangle and then shaded it in.

"You're really good at drawing," Kim said. "Thank you."

Jayna smiled. "And you're great at soccer. I'm glad we can help each other."

When Kim and Jayna started middle school, they weren't in any classes together and didn't share lunchtime either. They said hello in the hallway and played soccer together, but drifted apart as they made new friends. Now, they were enemies. She missed the days when they entertained their classmates and hung out in the park.

Up until last year, Jayna sometimes joined her, Charlotte, and Mason when they met at the park or mall. She added humor to their often serious conversations. When Jayna first joined Kim's soccer team, they were inseparable partners at practices. Near the end of last season, Jayna picked a new practice partner, without any explanation. Kim texted to find what went wrong, but Jayna ghosted her.

Now, Kim felt so alone. What she really wanted was to talk to her parents. Before they left, she was focused on staying behind and didn't want to give them any reason to change their mind. But the bullying escalated since they left and Kim felt lost. She decided to call. Kim glanced at the phone in her hand. Would Skype work? It would be late at night, but she decided to try. Tapping the app's icon, she scrolled until the picture of her mom appeared, and then tapped again. She heard the rhythmic beat as the call connected and then heard her mom's voice, groggy, but happy.

"Kim, this is a surprise. Is everything okay?" Kim's dad appeared behind her mom on the screen. He gave a quick wave before sitting down next to her mom.

Trying to blink back tears, Kim smiled. "Hi Dad. Everything is fine. I just miss you. Are you having a good time?"

Her mom smiled. "We miss you too. Grandma is reconnecting with friends she hasn't seen in forty-six years, and Dad is learning so much about his heritage. So far, it's been a good trip."

Her mom stifled a yawn, but Kim didn't want to hang up. She tried to think of something to keep her mom on the phone longer and decided to plunge ahead. "Um. Mom. Dad. I'm having trouble with a girl on my team. It's Jayna. She's turning the rest of the team against me and I don't know what to do." Kim tilted her head so her parents couldn't see her face.

Mom always said that she knew when Kim was upset by looking at her. "Do you know why? Maybe your coach can help."

Kim began pacing, phone in hand. "I wish I knew. I asked Coach Tim for help. He offered to talk to her, but I don't think that will help. She won't pass me the ball and gets everyone to ignore me."

Her dad scooched forward, his head filling the screen. "You only have another week until we return. Remember you made a commitment to your team and you chose to stay back for the playoffs. Just try to ignore Jayna at practice and she wouldn't dare try anything during your next game. If you're still having problems when we return, Mom and I can talk to Coach Tim."

Kim wanted to tell them about getting yelled at by the coach, Jayna pouring the drink in her lap, and arguing with Aunt Lang, but she didn't want to worry them. "I just need a day or two off soccer. Dad, could you call Aunt Lang and tell her I can skip practice tomorrow? Please." With the time change, they probably didn't realize she was missing today's practice while she talked to them.

On the screen, Kim could see her mom place a hand on her dad's shoulder and whisper something. He sighed. "We'll talk to Lang. You don't have to go tomorrow, but you do have to call Coach Tim to explain why you won't be at practice. You can't run away from your problems."

Kim breathed out in relief, and a day would buy her time and distance from Jayna. "Thanks, Mom and Dad. I'll figure it out. I love you." She tapped the End Call icon and the phone screen went blank just as Lang walked through the front door.

20 ~ Change of Heart 1977

Even though she just met Tran, Mai's heart felt like it was shattering as they walked back to the bus station. A dump truck screeched to a halt in front of them. People scattered to avoid the truck, and the cacophony of voices mixed with the rumble of the truck engine made it hard to hear. Three men jumped from the truck and placed orange cones in front of the station. "The bus station is closed," a man shouted as he shoved through the crowd and hopped into the truck.

People lined the edge of the street, waving their arms frantically to hail a taxi. As soon as a taxi pulled up, someone opened the door, and a group piled in. Taxi after taxi continued to arrive, load passengers, and depart.

Mai's panicked voice rose above the noise. "Lang, we need to get to Vung Tau before they close the shipping ports."

She watched Lang wave her arms to get the attention of a taxi driver. Before Lang could get to each taxi, somebody would push her aside and jump in. Mai held up her index finger and mouthed, "Wait" to Lang. Then she ran toward the alley.

"Don't leave me," Lang screamed, following Mai.

Racing to the back of the alley, Mai searched for Tran. She saw trash piled up, a discarded sofa, and rows of overflowing trash cans, but no little boy. Disappointed, she scanned the alley. As she hurried back toward the taxis, she heard loud hiccups coming from behind the sofa. Darting behind it, she spotted Tran, curled in a ball and sucking his thumb. Tears trickled down his dusty face. Mai bent down and scooped him into her arms. Holding him tightly, she motioned to Lang and then ran back to the sidewalk.

"This is a big mistake," Lang said, when they finally stopped in front of the bus station. The taxis were coming less frequently now, but the sidewalk remained crowded with people. "If we are going to get to Vung Tau Beach, we better go now." Another taxi pulled up and Lang leaned into the street, forcing the taxi to stop in front of her or hit her. Luckily, the taxi chose to stop. She opened the door, shoved her backpack inside and then got in. "Hurry up, Mai," she shouted. "Those ships will be filling."

Mai followed her into the taxi, clutching Tran in one arm and the handle to her backpack in the other. "Vung Tau—" Before she could finish her sentence, the taxi driver nodded, giving Mai the impression he made the trip many times in the past few days. Then he pulled out into the heavy traffic.

Lang stared ahead, her mouth set in a weary line. Mai looked at Lang and instantly felt a wave of regret. Why did she go back for Tran, knowing how difficult their journey would be? Their plan to move to the United States was a disaster and she had the feeling that things were going to get worse. The worry gave her a headache.

As Mai rubbed her fingers against her thumb, a habit she had whenever she was anxious, a small hand clutched one of her fingers. The other hand reached out and grasped Lang's finger. He smiled slightly at Mai, but his eyes remained large and sad. Lang tickled Tran's chin. He giggled and moved so he sat between them. The guilt lifted. Tran gave Mai hope that things would turn out all right.

21 ~ Keeping Secrets 2024

Kim stared at Aunt Lang, silently daring her to start another argument. But Lang didn't yell, argue, or even mention her running away. She just motioned for Kim to follow. Typical of Aunt Lang—avoid the issue, and it will go away.

When they got back to Grandma Mai's house, Lang's phone was ringing. Briefly, Kim worried that Lang would tell her parents she already missed a practice, but it was too late to do anything about that. The conversation between Aunt Lang and her dad was short and Lang frowned when she hung up. "Okay then. No practice tomorrow. First, you need to call your coach, apologize, and tell him why you weren't there today and won't be coming tomorrow." Then Lang walked out of the room.

Why did Aunt Lang feel so strongly about missing soccer practice? After discouraging Kim's enthusiasm for soccer for years, Lang should be celebrating that she wanted to quit. Throwing up her hands in exasperation, Kim flopped into a stiff burgundy chair in the corner of the room. She picked up her phone to call Coach and then put it down. Kim didn't want to bring up Jayna after she told him she could work it out. Finally, she just settled on offering a quick apology for missing practice and telling him that taking today and tomorrow off would improve her attitude. He wouldn't like that excuse, but at least it wasn't a lie.

Kim caught Coach Tim as he was driving home from practice. Anxiety rose in her throat like a thick knot.

"Kim, where were you today?"

Kim pushed ahead. "I'm sorry, Coach. I just needed some time off to, uh, to improve my game and attitude."

"A day off to improve your game? That doesn't make sense. And you control your own attitude. What's really wrong?"

There was silence on the line as Kim considered whether to bring up the bullying again. If it was just Jayna, Kim thought it would help to tell Coach, but the other girls were joining in. You couldn't fight a whole team. "I just need some time off to get my head straight so I can focus on the game."

Coach Tim sighed. "I can't hold a spot for you forever. There are a lot of girls who want to play forward. I see us winning the championship and we need you."

Kim told him she would be back in two days and then hung up before he had a chance to say more. She wandered around the house, picking up books and craft projects Lang had laying around. She began to stream a movie on her iPad but turned it off after a few minutes.

Aunt Lang came into the living room. "Did you call your coach?"

Kim nodded. "Yeah. He wasn't happy, but I think he understood."

Aunt Lang settled into her plump easy chair, pulled out her knitting needles, and continued working on another scarf for the long Wisconsin winters. Lang was always knitting a scarf, hat, or shawl that would keep her busy for hours.

Curiosity won out over the desire to not anger her. "Aunt Lang, why don't you like soccer?" They had all day, Kim reasoned, so why not learn a bit about her aunt?

"Who said I don't like soccer," Lang said. She stopped, knitting needles wound with loops of woolly yarn. "It is a sport that takes speed, determination, and a quick mind. Not many people can play soccer well. Do you have what it takes?"

Kim sat back, confused by what Lang meant. Her forehead furrowed when she thought about the effort she put into soccer. Was she trying hard enough? Kim thought about all the times she didn't run as fast as she could or didn't pay attention to the coach because she was talking to her teammates. How would Aunt Lang know that? Kim felt her cheeks flush with embarrassment.

A satisfied look spread across Lang's face as she sat there, clicking those darn knitting needles. Then Kim thought about the hours she practiced dribbling and outside kicks in her backyard, the time she spent at practices doing drills, and the competitive spirit she brought to every single game. Anger welled up in her chest. She folded her arms and glared at Aunt Lang. "What makes you a soccer expert?"

Lang put down her knitting and smirked at Kim. "You would be surprised at what I know."

It was almost as if Aunt Lang was taunting her. Realization spread over Kim like a beam of light. In the backyard, Lang gave suggestions for improving her game that could only be given by someone familiar with soccer. Maybe Lang watched soccer on TV or maybe she even played when she was her age, but that didn't seem possible. Why would she keep that a secret? She waited for Lang to continue, but instead, that satisfied smirk disappeared. Kim could tell the discussion was over. If Lang had secrets and wasn't going to share them, then she was going to figure them out on her own. Lang went back to knitting and Kim stomped upstairs.

At the top of the stairs, she looked around. All three bedroom doors were slightly ajar. The door to the ancient bathroom with its clawfoot tub was wide open. Then she noticed the fifth door at the end of the hallway that opened to the attic. Could there be something in the attic that would help her solve the Lang puzzle? Kim tiptoed over to the door and turned the handle.

The door slowly creaked open, revealing steep, narrow wooden stairs. The stairway was dark, and the air was hot and musty. Kim coughed as the dusty air filled her nose and mouth. Tentatively, she put her foot on the first step and it groaned under her weight. She gripped the railing and moved to the next step.

"Kim," Aunt Lang called from downstairs. She froze, worried that Lang knew she was climbing the hidden stairs. "Bring me the quilt on my bed. I feel a breeze."

Kim's shoulders dropped in relief. She quietly closed the door and retrieved the blanket from Lang's bedroom. Exploring the hidden staircase would have to wait until later.

22 ~ Escape From Vietnam 1977

An hour later, the taxi arrived at Vung Tau Beach. There were three ocean freighters lined up along the docks that could each hold hundreds of people. Refugees were milling about while others waited in lines to board the freighters. The warm air seemed to crackle with tension.

Mai, Tran, and Lang gathered their backpacks and stepped out of the taxi. After paying the driver, they stood in the ticket line, hoping to catch the next ship to anywhere. Mai secretly counted her remaining money while waiting. The taxi ride was expensive, and they would need additional money to pay Tran's passage. She was satisfied with how much they had left and was thankful Ba was so generous.

After hours of waiting, one of the ships blasted its horn, sending vibrations through the ground. Then it started its engines and roared away from the dock. Within minutes, the other ships repeated the blast of their horns and headed out to sea, leaving a tumble of waves behind. Mai expected to see more ships arrive, but the docks sat empty. Anticipation made her shaky. Would another ship come?

A soldier walked to the ticket booth and closed the shutters over the windows. Another soldier, with a buzz cut and lips curled into a sneer, stood on a box. "There are no more ships coming. Return to your homes immediately."

Lang turned toward Mai. "I'm tired and scared. Let's go home."

Mai reminded Lang how awful conditions were in Vietnam. Most likely, they would lose the store and playing football would be replaced by foraging for food. As Mai looked around, a man motioned to her. He was wearing baggy tan pants and a white silk shirt. A black leather pouch hung from his neck. Grabbing Tran with one hand and Lang with the other, she walked over to him.

The man looked around and then moved closer to her, keeping his voice low. He spoke in Vietnamese, but with a heavy accent that caused her to lean in and listen closely. "There is a boat waiting at the beach not far from here. For 500,000 dong, you can get on it. Indonesia is still welcoming refugees."

Mai looked down the shoreline in both directions. "I don't see a boat. How do I know you aren't just taking my money?"

"You'll need to trust me. Besides returning home, it is your only option." Mai looked at Lang, and she nodded. That was almost all the money Mai had. She pulled the money from her pocket and counted out 500,000 dong. He snatched the money and slid it into his pouch before anyone would notice, and she stuffed the few remaining dong deep in her pocket.

The man pointed down the beach. "Walk that way for half a kilometer and you will come to the Dinh river. A boat will be anchored in the sea directly out from where the river flows into the sea. You will need to wade out to it. Hurry. If the soldiers see, they will stop you."

She picked up Tran who was clutching her tunic and started walking down the beach. Lang followed. "Do you think this will work? Can we make it to the United States?" Lang said.

Mai shrugged. "From now on, we will have to depend on strangers to help us. I hope I picked the right stranger to trust."

The sun was dipping behind the rocky hills, leaving shadows on the beach. When they rounded a curve, a network of old wooden docks stretched out far into the sea, anchoring at least thirty fishing boats. Not far beyond the docks, a graying wooden boat about ten meters long and five meters wide bobbed in the water. She was surprised that it was much smaller than the freighters that just left and looked more the size of the tugboats that pulled those freighters to shore. A metal ladder hung from its side and a small cabin was perched in the middle. Heads peered out from the tall sides of the boat.

Mai looked at the water and then at Tran. "Hold on tight."

Dozens of people were scattered throughout the water, moving toward the boat. Mai waded into the warm brown water. She glanced back at Lang who stood still as a statue, watching them. Her racing heart slowed when she saw Lang heft her backpack above her head, like the people around her, and enter the water. At least ten more refugees followed.

As Lang caught up to Mai, the air echoed with the boom of a shotgun. "Halt," a voice screamed. "Do not move toward that boat. Get out of the water now!"

Mai jerked around and saw a soldier, standing on shore, gun raised.

23~ Waiting for the Right Time 2024

Kim carried the knit blanket downstairs and wrapped it around Aunt Lang's legs before dropping into the stiff upholstered chair across the room. She listened to the click of knitting needles as Lang wound the yarn around them. The minutes slowly ticked by.

Kim studied the road map of wrinkles at the corner of Lang's mouth. They gave an aura of sadness. Until her stay this week, she never thought about what made Lang so secretive and grumpy. But now, Aunt Lang was dropping little hints about herself, like tiny packages that were dying to be opened. Had she found a connection to her through soccer?

Aunt Lang's reluctance to share anything about her life invited questions, and there were other things Kim noticed. Lang had a stiff way of walking that caused her to limp when she was tired. She cooked fantastic Vietnamese food but wouldn't talk about her life in Vietnam. Finally, Lang watched a variety of television shows, then turned the TV off when a sporting event came on.

Should she, once again, incite Lang's wrath by being nosy? Yes. It was worth it, Kim decided. "Aunt Lang, when you were twelve, what did you like to do?"

Lang raised her head from her knitting. "My life was very different from yours. The Vietnam War had just ended and ..." Aunt Lang opened her mouth as if she wanted to say more, then closed it.

Kim tried one more time. "Were you in danger?" Just glancing at Aunt Lang told Kim that she went too far. A fire replaced the faraway look in her eyes and she pursed her lips.

"What happened in the past should stay there," Lang said, her voice barely above a whisper. Then she looked down and continued knitting. "Why don't you find something to do?"

Kim wasn't surprised at Aunt Lang's reaction but was disappointed she struck out on learning more about her. She went upstairs to read for a while, sure that Aunt Lang would fall asleep while she knitted.

After a while, Kim peeked downstairs and saw Lang stretched out on the couch, fast asleep. It was time to explore. Searching through the linen closet, Kim found a small flashlight. She turned it on and a bright light filled the hallway. She quickly shut it off. Without making a sound, Kim opened the attic door. Holding the flashlight in one hand and clinging to the railing leading upward, she gingerly put a foot on each bare wood step. Halfway up, a board groaned when she stepped on it. The wood bent almost to the point of breaking.

Worried the noise might summon Aunt Lang, Kim backed down the staircase and scurried into the living room where she was still dozing. Her legs were curled under her and the knitting needles had dropped to the floor. Lang's chest slowly rose and fell. Safe. Kim slipped back upstairs and climbed the attic staircase again. The stairs opened into a small room where a shaft of pale yellow light from a vent reached across to her. With one more large step, Kim entered the room and saw piles of boxes and old furniture.

Dust particles danced in the warm air. The warped plywood floor was yellowed, and the ceiling was so low that Kim couldn't straighten. She turned on the flashlight and moved it around the room like a spotlight from a search and rescue plane. Boxes were stacked to the ceiling. The corner held a blue velvet chair and matching ottoman, and an antique mirror with a crack across it filled another corner. A small black spider skittered along the edge of the wall and mouse droppings littered the floor.

Kim directed the beam of the flashlight on each box and noticed that almost all the boxes were labeled in big black letters with a Sharpie. Tax Returns. Photos. Old Receipts and Bills. Craft Projects. Football. Clothing. Letters …

With a start, Kim trained the flashlight beam on the box labeled Football to make sure what she read was correct. In Vietnam, soccer was called football. Could this be the missing link between Lang and her? The Letters box might be interesting too. Both boxes were at the bottom of the stacks.

Kim unstacked the boxes until she reached the ones she wanted. She wanted to open the Football box right there but resisted the urge and brought them downstairs in separate trips, balancing them against her chest. After the boxes were on the floor of her bedroom, she closed the door to the staircase and hurried back to her room.

Using a pair of scissors, Kim cut the tape on the box labeled Football and opened the flaps. On top was a blue T-shirt with the name "Kien" written across the back in thick black marker. Under the name was the number 6. Odd. It looked like a makeshift sports uniform. She started to lift the shirt out of the box, when Kim heard the tap tap of Aunt Lang's feet on the stairs.

How mad would Aunt Lang be if she caught Kim snooping? She didn't want to find out. Kim slid open her closet door and stuffed the boxes into it. Just as she closed the closet, Lang came in. "If you're going to be home all day, you might as well help me with some chores. The flower beds need weeding. Grab some garden gloves from the garage and you can start with the beds in the front yard."

Kim's heart stopped racing. The boxes were hidden, and Lang didn't notice anything wrong. Without a complaint, Kim breezed by Lang and headed out.

For the rest of the day, Aunt Lang kept Kim so busy that she didn't have time to open the boxes that were tucked in the closet. After weeding, Aunt Lang asked her to vacuum the hallway and empty the dishwasher. To Kim, it seemed that Lang's job was to make her so miserable that she would regret not going to soccer practice.

Late in the afternoon, Lang settled back down on the couch to continue with her knitting. Gleefully, Kim headed up to her bedroom. She opened the closet and carried the boxes to her bed. On the side of the box labeled "Football," there was a postmark from 1985, and a mailing label made out to Lang Kien at an unfamiliar address. The return address was from a place in Vietnam. She lifted out the shirt and saw a bundle of ribbons, like the ones Kim received at soccer tournaments, neatly tied together. The ribbons were all different colors and many of them had the outline of a soccer ball or soccer player on them. Although she couldn't read the writing, the dates ranged from 1975 to 1977. Could these be Aunt Lang's or Grandma Mai's? Neither of them ever talked about playing soccer.

The final item in the box was a tattered green scrapbook, stuffed so full that the binding was coming apart. Kim took it out of the box and set it in the desk in the corner of the bedroom. Sitting at the wobbly desk chair, she opened the cover of the scrapbook. Several ticket stubs and yellowed newspaper clippings fluttered out, somersaulted through the air, and landed on the floor. Kim picked them up and laid them on the desk.

Frustrated, Kim realized that she couldn't read any of the articles since they were written in Vietnamese, but she assumed they were about soccer since they had pictures of Vietnamese soccer players. She slipped the tattered newspaper clippings back in the scrapbook and turned the page. It held a black and white 8 x 10 photo of a group of girls and boys wearing shirts just like the one Kim found in the box. One tall, lanky girl standing off to the side and holding a soccer ball under her arm looked familiar.

There was a list of names under the picture. Starting at the back row, Kim used the index finger on her left hand to point to each name and the index finger on her right hand to point to each girl. When her finger landed on top of the familiar girl, Kim glanced down at her name: Lang Kien. She grinned. So Lang played soccer in Vietnam. This was the secret Aunt Lang was hiding. Why would Lang hide that she played soccer as a kid in Vietnam? Did Lang play soccer after she came to the United States? There must be more to this secret. Oh, how she wanted to talk to Lang and get some answers.

24 ~ Enemy on the Shore 1977

Fear made Mai freeze. The dozens of people surrounding her stood so still they looked like random wooden piers jutting out of the water. The soldier screaming for them to return was joined by two others who stood on shore in a line, shoulders touching. They raised their guns, pointing them at the people standing in the water. It seemed like a standoff, the soldiers' guns remaining trained on the refugees, until they turned and trudged back toward shore.

Mai turned toward the boat, knowing she had to make a quick decision. They were still about fifteen meters from it, but the water was only waist high, making it harder to hide. Tran clung to her chest like a baby monkey. "Lang, follow me."

"This is too dangerous. Please. We need to go back," Lang whispered. Mai glanced at Lang who turned toward shore like the others. Within seconds, she grabbed Lang's shoulders and twisted her toward the boat. Lang gasped as her backpack toppled out of her hands and into the water.

Before Lang could reach for her backpack, Mai grabbed her hand and pulled her forward. "Stay low and keep moving." The setting sun cast shadows in the water, and she counted on that to hide their movements. Although Lang scowled, she crouched so only her head and shoulders were above the water and headed toward the boat. Mai led, careful to keep Tran's head up and dry.

Mai hoped the soldiers would be so busy watching the exodus of people going toward them that they wouldn't notice them heading the other way. Most people headed towards shore, although a few, like them, continued toward the boat. As the boat grew closer and the shore further away, she quickened her pace. "We're almost there."

She slipped through the water, making ripples in a circle around them. Although the water was warm, Mai shivered. Tran laid his head against Mai and gripped her neck tighter as they continued, weaving to stay hidden behind the people who were headed in the opposite direction. Mai stood on her tiptoes to keep Tran's head above water. What would she do if it got any deeper? She sighed in relief when minutes later, they arrived at the boat where a sturdy metal ladder was attached to the side. Mai pried Tran's hands from around her neck and placed them on the ladder. "Climb," she said gently. "It's okay. I am right behind you."

Tran shook his head. Mai pushed his bottom upward, urging him up the ladder. He hesitated and tried to reach back, but she shook her head. Grabbing the side of the ladder, she began to climb, nudging Tran to move up each rung ahead of her. At last, a pair of arms reached down from the boat and pulled him in.

Water streamed from Mai's clothing as she climbed. Stopping momentarily, she looked down and saw Lang clinging to the bottom of the ladder. Halfway up, she heard shouts, and her heartbeat quickened when she realized the soldiers must have spotted them. "Stop," the soldier screamed. "Return to shore now or I'll shoot."

Mai heard the thud of Lang's feet on each rung as she clambered up. The air grew deathly silent, heads that were peering over the side of the boat disappeared, and even the birds stopped swooping low. Refugees still in the water turned and waded back to shore. Mai didn't move up or down the ladder, indecision paralyzing her. Now it was Lang's turn to take control. "Hurry," Lang said. "We can make it. Go."

Lang's voice startled Mai who continued climbing until several arms reached over the side of the boat and pulled her in. As soon as they put her down, Tran wrapped his arms tightly around Mai's leg. A shot blasted from the shore, followed by a parade of gunfire a few seconds later. The air filled with smoke and the sulfur smell of gunfire. Bullets looked like popcorn sizzling in a pan as they landed, leaving sprays in the air.

Mai looked over the side, holding her breath, and watched Lang climb the last few rungs. Another shot echoed in Mai's ears. She heard Lang scream and saw her lose her footing on the ladder. Two men reached over the boat and grasped Lang's arms to keep her from falling back into the dark and foamy water. Then another man reached over, grabbed the back of Lang's shirt, and pulled her in.

The gunfire stopped as the men lowered Lang to the floor of the boat, and then erupted again. Lang was breathing hard, her chest rapidly rising and falling. She sat with her back propped against the wooden side of the boat and groaned each time it lurched up and down in the rolling waves. Her body shook, splaying the salty ocean water everywhere. Blood seeped through her silken pants and puddled on the ground. Lang grimaced. "Ah, my leg. I've been shot."

Mai slipped down next to Lang, and pressed her hands against Lang's leg, hoping to stop the bleeding. It seeped through her fingers and the circle of blood on Lang's pant leg widened. The boat was crowded, and everyone huddled in groups, attempting to protect themselves from the bullets by placing backpacks and boxes on top of themselves. Mai realized nobody would be able to help until the gunfire ended and the boat left harbor. She held onto Tran with one hand and continued applying pressure to Lang's injured leg with the other. Then she waited.

25 ~ Enemy on the Field 2024

Kim reluctantly went back to soccer practice the next day, but her mind was on Aunt Lang and the box. Coach Tim smiled when he saw her walking along the sideline. She expected him to be a bit grumpier after taking two practices off. "Good to have my star player back. Did you and Jayna work things out?"

"No. If anything, it's gotten worse." Kim gave a half-smile, but then her lips flattened when she saw Jayna glaring at her. A ripple of worry made her stomach hurt.

Coach Tim surveyed the field, but by then, Jayna was talking with a group of friends. "It's time the three of us sit down and talk. How about after practice?"

After the soda incident at the mall, Kim didn't want to talk to Jayna, but how could she say no? It would look like she wasn't trying to solve the problem. "I guess so."

Kim joined her team on the soccer field. She felt a little better, convinced that maybe Coach really could fix the problem. During practice, Jayna was on her best behavior. She didn't call her any names, and even passed the ball to her once.

After practice, Coach Tim caught up with Jayna. "Let's talk." Jayna followed him to the bench, and he motioned for Kim. Jayna turned her head toward Kim, her eyes shooting beams of hatred. Kim pretended like she didn't see Jayna's glare and hurried to catch up to them.

When Jayna sat down, Kim was careful to sit a foot from her. Coach Tim looked down at them. "Jayna, I've noticed you're not always playing fair with Kim during practices."

Jayna scrunched her forehead. "What do you mean?"

Coach Tim stared at Jayna for a moment, as if deciding what to say. "Come on, Jayna. What's up?"

Jayna hung her head. "I dunno. It's just that I have to fight to get Kim to pass me the ball. I'm tired of it, so I've been doing the same thing to her. I think she's a little jealous since I've improved so much." She added a long, dragged-out sigh.

Kim's jaw dropped. How could Jayna lie like that? "Jayna, that's not true. I pass the ball to you as much as anyone else. We used to be friends, but you've turned the whole team against me."

Jayna squeezed a tear from her eye. "Coach, the team is just backing me up. They know that Kim doesn't like me. She's causing problems for the whole team, not just me."

Confused, Coach Tim looked at both girls. Kim glared at Jayna and then turned to Coach Tim. "It's happening on and off the field. A few days ago, she dumped an entire soda in my lap at the mall."

Jayna smirked. "That was an accident."

The tips of Coach Tim's fingers rested on his forehead. There was a pause where he seemed to be collecting his thoughts. "Girls, we're a team and you both need to play like you're part of it. Do you think you can put your personal feelings aside?"

Jayna looked at Coach, wiped away a tear, and smiled. "Sure. I'm sorry, Kim. I really am."

Anger bubbled up in Kim's chest. It took her a minute to rein it in and not say anything. Coach stared at her. "Kim? How 'bout it? For the good of the team?"

"Sure," she said. "For the good of the team."

Coach Tim smiled. "Why don't you two shake hands? It's a fresh start beginning today."

Kim held out her hand. She wanted to show Coach that she wasn't the problem. Jayna took her hand and shook it, the edges of her lips turning up. That couldn't have gone any worse, Kim thought. That devious sneak got away with it again. She grabbed her duffel bag and headed toward the parking lot. Jayna followed.

"As soon as they were out of earshot of Coach Tim, Jayna moved beside Kim and thrust her head close to Kim's ear. Tattletale," she hissed. "Coach may be watching on the field, but he can't protect you all the time. Make things easy on yourself and quit."

Kim walked away, but Jayna's evil laugh followed. Her anger was replaced by the heavy feeling of defeat. She spotted Aunt Lang's car parked along the fence where she was watching the practice, and realized Lang often watched her soccer practices from a distance. One more thing that confirmed Kim's suspicion that Lang knew more about soccer than she let on. She threw her bag in the back and slumped in the front seat. Lang turned to Kim. "You did well today, and it looked like Jayna left you alone."

"No, she didn't. Now Jayna is just really careful to make sure nobody sees her bullying. I've tried. I give up. I quit."

Kim looked out the window and refused to say anything else, so Aunt Lang pulled out of the parking lot and drove home. Once home,

Kim dropped her duffel bag inside the door and started up the stairs. Lang followed. "Sometimes you can't give up. No matter how hard things get, no matter who tries to get in your way, you have to keep your goal in sight. Do you still *want* to play soccer?"

Kim shrugged. "I love the action, strategy, friends, and the cheering crowds." Then she frowned. "But Jayna is making me miserable, and it's even worse to be ignored by everyone on my team. I just can't go back now or maybe ever."

Lang followed Kim into the bedroom. "There was a time when I was discouraged and gave up. I should have followed my dream, but it shattered, and I refused to pick up the pieces. I regret that now. I don't want that to happen to you."

Was Lang filling in some pieces to the puzzle? Could this be tied to the scrapbook? Kim plunged ahead with the question she'd been wanting to ask. "Did your dream have to do with soccer? Did you play soccer when you lived in Vietnam?"

Lang drew in a deep breath. "Why would you ask that?" Her words were spoken slowly, syllable by syllable, and her voice sounded cold as a winter wind. Kim knew she went too far but continued anyway.

"I found a box in the attic. It contained a shirt, ribbons, and a scrapbook. The scrapbook had a newspaper article with your name in it. There was a picture….."

Lang's hands clenched in angry balls and her face turned red. "You had no right to invade my privacy. Some things are better left in the past," Flecks of spit rocketed from her lips like tiny shards of glass. "Where is that box?"

Kim retrieved the boxes from the closet. An old scrapbook shouldn't make Lang so angry, Kim reasoned. She wasn't being fair. One minute she was kind and full of advice and the next minute, Lang was hateful and secretive. First Coach Tim's lack of support and then this. Kim had enough. She hefted both boxes into Lang's arms. The weight of the boxes made Lang take a step backwards.

Not knowing what to say next, Kim ran out of the house, slamming the door loudly behind her.

26 ~ Survival 1977

To Mai's relief, the gunfire stopped, and the dusky sky was silent. Two men worked furiously to pull up the thick rope holding a heavy slab of metal that anchored the boat to the sandy bottom. Lang's soft moans prompted Mai to seek help. She pulled her bloodied hand away from Lang's leg. "Is there a doctor on board?"

Groups huddled together, watching Mai move around the crowded boat, bumping into people while begging for help. She pulled Tran along, tightly gripping his hand. The men finished bringing up the anchor, the engine hummed to life, and the boat slowly backed out amid a new volley of gunfire.

A man holding a handgun stood at the bow. Hoping that he was in charge, she moved toward him. "Please help my sister. I think she's been shot."

"Get down," the man shouted. "They will keep shooting until we are out of sight." He raised his gun, pointing it toward shore.

Mai ducked down so her head was lower than the side of the boat and blinked away the tears. She always told herself crying never helps, but she felt helpless and alone, even though she was surrounded by at least 100 people. A loud noise echoed in Mai's ears. Smoke wafted from the man's gun and the smell of sulfur mixed with diesel hung in the air. As the boat turned around and rumbled toward the open sea, she raised her head and saw the young soldier, who had been shooting at them laying on the ground. The gunfire stopped and the man tucked the gun in his pocket before looking around. "It's a miracle there are no bullet holes in the boat."

Mai and Tran rushed back to Lang. "I'm here. Please be okay." Mai pushed Lang's pant leg up, causing her to draw her injured leg in and scream. The bullet hole just above Lang's knee oozed blood. A man with a tan safari hat covering black hair skimming his shoulders came forward. "I was a medic in the army," he said. "Maybe I can help."

The man was slim and not much taller than Mai. He had a narrow face and long, elegant fingers. Lang groaned when he bent down next to her and straightened her bleeding leg. He used his fingers to press near the bullet hole. Then he lifted her leg slightly and felt under it. "The bullet went cleanly through her leg."

Lang was a ghostly shade of gray. The man scanned the crowd gathered in a semicircle around him. "We need bandages."

"Would cloth strips do?" an older man asked, removing his gray button-down shirt. The medic nodded, and Mai felt a rush of gratitude that a stranger offered his own shirt. Somebody handed a pocketknife to the man, who pierced the shirt with it, making a short tear. Then he ripped it into thick strips and handed them to the medic.

A man with a wide-brimmed bucket hat stepped through the crowd. "Here's a first aid kit," he said, handing it to the medic. Then he disappeared.

Opening the kit, the medic took out a bottle of alcohol and poured half of it over Lang's wounds. She cried out, but didn't move. Next, he painted iodine around the edges of the wound with a tiny brush and wrapped the strips of cloth tightly around her leg. The bleeding slowed and then finally stopped. The medic frowned at Mai. "The bullet entered her leg just above the back of the knee and it seems to have missed the bone when exiting. That is fortunate. It will take time to heal, but she will survive. When we get to Indonesia, a doctor can take care of her."

Mai stifled a cry of relief. "Thank you. I'm so grateful you were here to help."

The medic returned supplies to the first aid kit, tucked it under his arm, and headed toward the cabin on the boat. The crowd dispersed, settling back into their small groups, and the boat cut through the gentle waves as it headed out to sea.

Mai sat, wrapping an arm around Tran and resting her other hand on Lang's shoulder. The sky sparkled with a golden spray of stars. Mai looked around the boat. The worn wooden sides were tall, and the floor was made of rough sawn planks. The small cabin was surrounded by boxes filled with crackers and rice, large milk jugs full of water, and fishing poles. A steering wheel the size of a wagon wheel was mounted behind the cabin. Looking through gaps in the groups of people, she spotted metal buckets along the front of the boat holding additional supplies. Almost every inch of the floor was taken up by supplies or people.

Lang rested, her mouth slightly open. Tran laid his head against Mai and popped his thumb in his mouth. Mai smiled at him before resting her head against the side of the boat to sleep.

27 ~ The Runaway 2024

After fleeing Lang's house, Kim ran down the sidewalk and across busy streets. Anger and loneliness made her heart swell until it hurt. She didn't mean to make Lang angry by snooping in the attic. It was just that Kim was excited she and Aunt Lang finally had a connection, something in common.

Eventually, Kim's pace slowed until she walked aimlessly down a street lined with small shops, not sure where to go or what to do. Calling Charlotte or Mason wouldn't work because she forgot to grab her phone. She was hungry, but didn't have money to buy a burger at Charley's Grill either. Miserable, Kim kept her head bent low while she trudged along the sidewalk. She walked past Pizza Haven where the scent of spicy sauce teased her nose. Her stomach knotted up, part from hunger and part from the stress of arguing with Jayna and Aunt Lang. She walked along the empty sidewalk, thinking. Maybe she should go back to her own house? It would be so nice to curl up in her own bed and shut out the rest of the world for a while.

Kim turned around to head home. Then she stopped. Aunt Lang found her there before. Most likely, Lang was sitting in the living room, waiting for her to walk through the door. No. She wouldn't give Aunt Lang the satisfaction of seeing her return home so soon. Kim hung her head and continued her lonely walk.

If Mom and Dad were home, they would understand why I went into the attic. They would help me deal with Jayna, and I wouldn't have run away, she thought, feeling sorry for herself. Just thinking about Jayna made Kim's anger flare. She couldn't believe Jayna told Coach Tim she wasn't being a team player.

The sun was low now and surrounded by a purple haze. The night was warm and fireflies flashed their yellow lights in the darkening sky. Kim continued walking, her feet automatically taking her to the soccer field. She created such a mess by refusing to go to Vietnam, being nosy, and not dealing with Jayna's bullying from the start. Her life was a jumble of people and events that pulled her apart from the inside.

Kim wasn't sure how much time passed, but it was dark by the time she reached the soccer field. The humid air cooled and the night grew silent. Crickets stopped their high pitched chirp, the firefly lights were sporadic, and the stars glistened in the sky like teardrops. Kim slumped against a bench and enjoyed the silence.

Soft weeping broke through the comfort of the quiet night. Refusing to believe her ears, Kim didn't move, content to rest her tired feet. When the crying didn't stop, even after ignoring it for a long time, she forced herself to stand and follow the sad sound. Walking the length of the soccer field, she ended up at a short cement building butting up against the bleachers. Parents sold hotdogs, popcorn and sugary Pixie Stix out of the building during games.

The crying turned to short gasps and seemed to be coming from the top row of the bleachers. Kim quietly climbed the bleachers and spotted a girl with hair weaved into two long braids, her head resting on knees that were bent toward her chest. She froze, trying to decide whether to approach the girl or give her privacy. The cries became softer until she could barely hear them and then crescendoed into loud wails. Would the girl be mad that someone found her? It didn't seem right to just leave. She walked closer. "Hello. Are you all right?"

The weeping stopped and the girl lifted her head, while wiping her tears. Kim gasped. "Jayna?"

Following the crying was a mistake, Kim thought. Once again, she shouldn't put her nose where it didn't belong, and she certainly didn't want to be involved with Jayna's problems. She had enough of her own. Jayna must not have heard her, because she put her head back down and continued to sob, taking in big gulps of air and then hiccuping. Looking at her curled on the stadium bleacher made Kim's heart soften. Maybe Jayna needed a friend now? Should she help? Her heart said "Yes," but her brain screamed "No." Especially after the food court failure. But, what a coincidence they both ran away tonight and ended up at the soccer stadium together.

"Jayna, It's me ... Kim. Are you okay?"

Jayna raised her head. Her eyes frosted over, and a corner of her mouth curled up in a sneer. "Get out of here! Leave me alone."

Kim stepped back. She thought about the time that Jayna emptied her water bottle after a hot practice, the soda dripping from her lap, and the team gathering at the ice cream shop without her. Rage welled up in her. Kim turned around and stomped down the bleacher stairs and onto the edge of the field. Her fists clenched and her chest felt heavy, making it hard to breathe. The grass was damp and quickly soaked through her shoes as she walked across the field.

Jayna's constant pranks and sly comments. Mom and Dad's absence just when she needed them the most. Her teammates watching Jayna bully her without saying a word. Lang, always frowning, spouting critical, stinging remarks. Kim felt like her head was going to explode, like a volcano releasing all its heat and pressure. By the time she got to the other side of the field, the stomping turned into a slow walk. Kim's breathing evened and her hands relaxed. She thought it must be awful to be Lang or Jayna. Neither were ever happy. Lang was always angry and Jayna plain mean.

Kim stopped mid step. Dad always said you have to get inside a bully's head to figure her out. Since her parents said she had to go to practices, maybe she needed to get inside Jayna's head. She decided to take Dad's advice. Turning around, Kim headed back toward the bleachers.

28 ~ The Journey Begins 1977

The next day, Mai woke up and immediately hung her head over the boat before throwing up. The inside floor and walls of the boat emanated with the smell of decaying fish and sea water. That, along with the motion as it rose and fell in the waves, made Mai nauseous. She focused on the horizon to help settle her stomach. A gentle wind helped the boat cut through the silvery waves that reached out like icy fingers.

The man with the bucket hat, who supplied the first aid kit, appeared beside her. He had piercing dark eyes, full lips, and towered at least a full head above her. Although he looked only a few years older than Mai, she saw a quiet confidence in him. He handed her a piece of folded rice paper filled with crackers. "It will take a day or two for you to get used to the sea. Until then, nibble on crackers."

Mai was embarrassed that he saw her vomiting, but he didn't seem surprised. "Thank you. I'm already feeling better. I'm Mai, and this is Lang, and Tran," she said, pointing.

"I'm Duc and this is my boat," he said, proudly waving his hand in front of him as if introducing a person. He looked down at Lang. "How is she?"

Mai peered at Lang, who was sleeping fitfully. "I don't know. The medic said, luckily, the bullet didn't break a bone." Broken bone or not, it was still awful.

"The trip to Indonesia will take about a week, if all goes well. When we arrive, a doctor can look at it."

Mai looked startled. "If all goes well? What can go wrong?"

Before Duc had a chance to answer, somebody from the other side of the boat called for him. He offered a quick wave. "A captain never rests. I'll stop by later."

***

On the third day, Mai's stomach settled as she got used to the rhythm of the waves. The boat moved quickly through the turbulent water, but the days seemed long. She looked forward to the time Duc spent with her, talking about his life as a fisherman and helping refugees. He told her how he secretly smuggled hundreds of gallons of fresh water and other supplies on board. "Each night, for weeks before this trip, I filled containers with water and used a wagon to carry them to my boat along with crackers, fishing poles, and bait. It was only on the darkest nights, when the moon was hidden behind clouds, that I dared do this." His confidence reassured her.

Duc was kind and funny, and Mai felt a surge of joy when he stopped by to talk. While he worked, Mai and Tran spent the long, hot day talking to other passengers, playing hand-clap games, and telling stories. Tran loved to listen to stories about superheroes and dragons that Mai made up. As a three-year old, he had an impressive vocabulary, but Tran refused to talk about life on the street or the mother who gave him up. Sometimes, when Mai asked too many questions, Tran covered her mouth with shaky hands.

Throughout the day, Lang was listless, but occasionally cried out. Mai held a cup to Lang's mouth, encouraging her to drink. She broke off a piece of cracker and tried to place it on Lang's tongue. "You have to eat," Mai coaxed. Lang turned her head and pushed her away. The most difficult battle was helping Lang squat over a big tin bucket to go to the bathroom, a task Tran loved.

Mai was relieved when the medic stopped by that evening to look at Lang's leg. He frowned as he gently pressed near the wound."Your sister's wound is healing so I'm surprised she is still in so much pain. Make sure she drinks enough and let her sleep as much as she wants since it will make the time pass quickly."

***

The fourth day of their voyage started with a pale blue sky cradling wispy white clouds. Mai and Tran ate rice, raw fish, and a cup of water for breakfast, and Duc joined them as they ate. "We are fortunate. The sea is calm, and we have enough supplies. We would have run out of food if some people weren't forced to return to shore."

Tran plopped down on Duc's legs, begging him to move up and down in a game of horsey. Duc bumped his sturdy legs up and down and Tran giggled. Mai studied Duc as he played with Tran. He had the broad shoulders and the calloused hands of a fisherman. His almond-shaped eyes twinkled when he was talking to them, but she noticed they were thin slits when he was dealing with a problem. Her heart beat a little faster when she watched him.

"Why do you do this?" Mai asked when Tran darted off to play with the group of older boys. Duc looked at Mai, started to say something, and then hesitated. "You don't have to talk," Mai interrupted. "You look so tired. Why don't you sleep now while I organize the food and supplies?"

Duc settled back to nap for a while. When he woke, he didn't get up, but instead, began to tell his story. "Last year, I used this boat to take my parents, little sister, grandma, uncles, and aunts to Thailand. My father worked with the American government to get supplies to the South Vietnamese troops. When North Vietnam took over, my family was punished because he helped the Americans. We were assigned to a reeducation camp in North Vietnam where we would be forced to do hard labor until we accepted the new communist government. Instead, we chose to escape."

Tran returned to Mai and curled up in her lap. His thumb found its way into his mouth, as usual, and his chubby fingers wrapped around her hair. Duc smiled at them. "A storm rolled in on the third day, and my family was terrified. The wind whipped waves against the side of my boat so hard that it felt like we were a paper boat sailing in a puddle during a downpour. My boat began to take on water and list to one side, and I was sure it would sink."

Duc sat up straighter. "Just when I thought we were all going to drown, a large boat came alongside us. The boat was crowded, but the captain helped me and my family come aboard. Then he tied my boat behind his and took us to Thailand. We wouldn't have survived if it weren't for that kind captain."

Mai looked at Duc, puzzled. "What happened to your family? Why aren't you in Thailand?"

"My family is safe. They found jobs and are working to save enough money to travel to Australia. I am thankful the boat captain was willing to take on more passengers than his boat could hold. Now it's my turn to return the favor by helping others escape."

Mai's admiration for Duc grew. "Who is the man who told us about your boat?"

Duc smiled. "That man is my cousin. He collects money to pay for the supplies and food for the journey, and to take care of his family. It is dangerous work and if the soldiers catch him, he would be sent to prison. After finding enough people to fill my boat, he disappears into the crowd, being careful the soldiers don't notice him."

Mai was touched by Duc's kindness. He could have charged much more money than he did. Looking at him, she saw bravery and compassion. After finishing his story, Duc got up to hand out fishing poles so the men could catch the next meal. Later in the day, while Mai watched Duc work, his eyes turned to thin slits. The winds died, which meant the old engine had to do more work, and the boat slowed. She wondered if that was one of the things Duc worried would go wrong.

Wanting to share Duc's story, she nudged Lang. Lang groaned, but didn't move. Her cheeks were hot and dry, and her leg quivered. Mai unwrapped the makeshift bandage and saw red streaks starting at the wound and moving away from it like little arrows. Mai's fear rose like a giant winged dragon when she saw the fiery red streaks. Infection. She wondered if Lang would survive, and guilt consumed her. Life on the street or in a reeducation camp in Vietnam was better than no life at all.

29 ~ Endless Night 2024

Each step Kim took as she climbed the bleacher stairs made a metallic echo that bounced around the stadium, warning Jayna she was returning. She could hear hiccupping and an occasional sniff as she approached.

"Go away," Jayna said, but it came out soft as a whisper. She lowered her head and continued to cry.

Kim wondered what she should do. It seemed like Jayna was beyond despair, and Kim knew that she wasn't the person to comfort her. Besides, her anger at Jayna was still bubbling close to the surface and it was hard to contain it. Indecision paralyzed Kim. Time passed while Jayna cried, and she watched her in uncomfortable silence. The sky grew darker, and the stars seemed to slide back into it as if covering themselves with a blanket. A sliver of a pale moon rose higher in the sky.

Finally, compassion overtook annoyance and Kim sat down beside Jayna. Instead of spitting out another hateful comment, Jayna leaned on her, the way Kim leaned on her mother when she needed comforting. She put her arm around Jayna and eventually, the sobbing stopped, but not before Kim's shoulder was wet from tears.

"I'm sorry you're so sad," Kim said. She felt awkward, sitting beside her enemy. Jayna gulped huge mouthfuls of air before finally looking up. She gave Kim a soft smile.

Jayna wiped away her tears. "Why are you here? I'm surprised you didn't run away when you saw me. I've been awful to you."

Kim shrugged, not sure what to say. Jayna had been awful to her, and she was worried the same mean girl would return any minute now. Curiosity won out. Instead of answering Jayna's question, she asked, "Why are you here?"

"I told my parents again that I wanted to quit soccer," Jayna said. "Finally, they were really considering it until my grandpa slammed his fist on the table and yelled at me for disappointing him. I just couldn't take it anymore and ran away."

"Again? Finally?" Kim repeated. The conversation was getting stranger and more confusing. Jayna loved soccer. She was so lucky her parents, grandparents, aunts, uncles and cousins came to every single game to cheer her on. They were a happy, loud group that clearly loved watching Jayna play. It didn't make sense that she wanted to quit. Kim wished she had a big family who loved soccer. Sure, her parents came to every game, but Grandma rarely did. And Jayna's grandpa had such a passion for soccer while Aunt Lang hated it.

Jayna brushed her damp hair from her face. "When I was nine, my grandpa talked me into playing soccer. I really wanted to take art classes, but Grandpa thought I would be good at soccer, so I agreed to play to make him happy. That's when I asked you to help me. I've been playing ever since, but each year, I hate it more and more. I'm pretty good and it makes my grandpa happy to watch me, but I'm miserable."

Kim thought about how different their families were. "What do your parents think?"

Jayna threw her head back. "They want me to play because it makes Grandpa happy. They think it would be disrespectful to him if I quit."

"Why does your grandpa care if you play soccer, take art lessons, or do something else?" Kim thought about how her parents supported her but wouldn't get upset if she quit. It was late, and she shivered in the soft breeze. She removed her arm from Jayna's shoulder.

Jayna sat up straighter. "My grandpa wanted my dad to be a pro soccer player, but he had bad asthma as a kid and couldn't run. So now my grandpa is obsessed with the idea that I will be the next Samantha Kerr or Mia Hamm. I play soccer for him." Jayna leaned back against the bleachers.

"Grandpa was a great soccer player and went to college on a soccer scholarship. His teammates came from all over the world—Asia, Europe, South America, the United States. He always talks about how good the Asian and South American soccer players on his team were."

Kim was confused. "So what does that have to do with you?"

"Grandpa talks about how he worked so hard to be better than the players from other countries. Grandma says he had a chip on his shoulder because he had to be the best. At the last game of his junior year, Grandpa broke his leg when two players coming from opposite directions collided with him. His leg never healed well enough to play again."

Kim interrupted. "So he wants you to be the next great soccer player since he couldn't?" She was incredulous that Jayna's grandpa put so much pressure on her and felt thankful she didn't have that pressure. Then she thought of the pressure Aunt Lang put on her the last few days.

Tears ran down Jayna's cheeks, catching at the corners of her nose and top of her mouth. "He constantly talks about his favorite women's soccer players and says I can be better than any Asian or South American player. He says I'll be famous one day. I'm afraid to tell him that's not what I want."

Jayna got up and paced back and forth across the row of bleachers in front of Kim. "My grandpa watches you closely because you're part Asian and the best soccer player on the team. On the way home, he talks about how well you played. Every single game, he compares me to you and he always says that if I work hard enough, I can be better than you. I think he wishes you were his granddaughter instead of me."

Kim stared at Jayna, surprised, and her mouth opened into a silent O. "Is that why you're so mean to me?"

Jayna sat next to Kim. "Soccer comes so easy to you, and I can tell you love it. You're lucky that you never have a big crowd of loud, embarrassing people at every game who cheer too much when you finally get the ball and grumble when you make a bad play. I thought if I could get you to quit, maybe Grandpa wouldn't be so hard on me."

Kim felt a flicker of anger. It made sense that she was mad at her, but it wasn't fair that Jayna bullied her for something she couldn't control. Kim felt lucky she could just play soccer because she loved it. The only pressure on her was from herself. Her parents didn't care if she missed the ball or lost a game. It must be terrible to feel like you couldn't make a mistake without everyone judging you. The flicker of anger died.

Jayna hung her head. "I feel awful. I even called you a gook. Grandpa uses that word when he watches international games. My mom told me what it means and gets mad when Grandpa says it. I'm so sorry. I wouldn't blame you if you hate me."

Did just saying sorry make Jayna think that everything was okay now? The anger made her cheeks burn. "Well, you succeeded. I decided to quit."

Jayna sucked in a breath. "Kim, please don't quit. I'll make this right. I'll tell Coach Tim what I've been doing."

"I don't know if that's enough. The kids on our team hate me now. I was just as miserable as you this season."

"Is that the reason why you ran away?" Jayna said.

Kim shook her head and shared her story about Aunt Lang. It was Jayna's turn to be surprised. "Why would your aunt change from a soccer player to a soccer hater?"

Kim shrugged. "Maybe we can trade your grandpa for my aunt."

The tension broke when Kim giggled. Jayna laughed too. They scooted closer together and strategized how they could convince Jayna's grandfather to allow her to try something else. They whispered, cried, laughed, and linked arms. The night grew brighter, the moon rose higher in the sky, and the stars twinkled like tiny shards of glass. It felt like old times, and that felt good.

30 ~ Endless Days 1977

"Help me. Where's the medic?" Mai pleaded. She gathered Lang in her arms and hugged her tightly. Lang's wound oozed a thin line of watery blood and beads of sweat glistened on her forehead. "Please ..."

The medic appeared, followed by Duc who carried the first aid kit. They laid Lang flat on her back and the medic examined her seeping wound. He drew in a breath and then searched through gauze, bandages, and aspirin before finding the alcohol. As Lang screeched, he used it to clean the wound, brush it with more iodine, and wrap it again.

Even though the day was hot, Mai's panic turned her heart cold. She clutched Lang's arm with one hand while wiping her damp forehead with the other. Tran nudged closer to Mai, whimpering. The medic finished his work. "Her leg is infected. The next twenty-four hours are most critical. With luck, the infection will clear."

Mai nodded, feeling grateful for the medic. She didn't want to ask what would happen if the infection got worse and she sensed he didn't want to tell her.

The next day stretched endlessly with the sun climbing higher and burning down on the refugees. Most of them leaned against the side of the boat or curled up on the floor, dozing. Mai sat next to Lang, holding her hand and wiping her forehead with a cloth wet with sea water. Tran curled next to Mai, sleeping through the steamy, lazy afternoon. She put a cup of water to Lang's lips and made her drink, and then fell asleep next to Lang.

When Mai woke, the air felt cool, and the sky was filled with a million tiny stars flickering like sparks from a fire. Sometime during the heat of the long afternoon, Tran moved from Mai's lap and was stretched out on his stomach next to her. Should she have brought Tran with them? Duc told her the journey could be dangerous and they still had three more days to travel. At least on the streets of Vietnam, Tran was able to beg for food. What right did she have to take a small boy and twelve-year old Lang across an ocean to a strange land thousands of miles away?

Mai placed her hand on Tran's back. He turned over. His thumb temporarily left his mouth, and the corners turned up in a slight grin. "*Yêu bạn*," Tran whispered.

She smiled at him and tousled his hair. "I love you too, Tran." Mai was amazed that Tran could be happy. Maybe bringing him with them would give Tran the opportunity for a better life. At least he had somebody who loved him and cared for him. She felt comforted by that.

Mai reached out her other hand and placed it on Lang's forehead. Instead of the sweaty, sticky heat that she expected, Lang's forehead was cool. The fever broke. "Lang?" Mai said tentatively.

Lang opened her eyes. She grimaced but pulled herself to a sitting position. Mai wanted to ask Lang how her leg was feeling, but she was afraid to hear the answer. Lang wiggled her toes and then drank from the cup that was sitting beside her before nibbling the crackers Mai saved for her. "My leg doesn't throb anymore. I was so scared."

Mai hugged Lang. "So was I." Between Tran's crooked smile and Lang's hopeful words, Mai's panic subsided. In a few days, they would be off the boat and on their way to America.

31 ~ Caught
2024

Kim and Jayna sat together, planning how they were going to get Jayna out of being on the team. "Maybe you should play so badly that Coach Tim will have to cut you," Kim suggested.

Jayna laughed. "My grandpa would figure that plan out before Coach had a chance."

Kim nodded.

"What if I faked a sprained ankle?" Jayna said.

Kim shook her head. "Sprained ankles heal. Then you'll be right back on the team." Their voices rose as their ideas grew sillier and their laughter more often. It felt so good to be laughing again.

During a brief silence, Kim looked at the sky. "I wonder how late it is. I forgot my phone and I'm sure Aunt Lang is wondering where I am."

Jayna pulled her phone from her pocket and tapped it. "It's after midnight." She tapped a few more times and then drew in a breath. "My mom keeps texting me asking me to come home. I'm just not ready yet, but they sure are going to be mad when I do go back."

Kim gulped. She hadn't thought about how mad or worried Aunt Lang was going to be. "I need more time too."

Jayna's phone darkened. In the quiet, Kim heard soft footsteps. She turned to Jayna and put a finger to her lips. At that moment, someone shined a bright light, causing her to see glaring spots.

"Security! What are you doing here?"

Kim tried to follow the voice, but the flashlight shining in her eyes made it hard to see. She thought of how reckless she had been by running away and hiding out at the soccer field, and regret sat heavy in her chest. "W-W-We're just talking."

A man pointed the flashlight away from them and the spots floating in front of Kim's eyes disappeared, allowing her to get a closer look at him in the dim light. He was tall with shaggy hair that touched the collar of his button down shirt. His rough skin and crooked frown made him look like the scarecrow in The Wizard of Oz, but scarier.

The man stood next to them, blocking their escape. "You're trespassing. The city hired me to catch the kids who've been vandalizing the stadium. I bet you're the ones who spray painted the bathroom doors last week."

Indignant, Kim stood up. "We're just sitting here, talking, and I don't know anything about spray painting bathroom doors. I'm sorry. We'll leave." She couldn't believe she felt brave enough to talk back to the security guard, but she didn't like being accused of vandalism.

Kim turned to leave, but the guard grabbed her wrist, forming an O like a handcuff. Alarmed, she tried to pull her wrist back, but his rough hands were large and strong.

"You aren't going anywhere." He was breathing hard. The man pulled a small remote control out of his pocket. With four button pushes, the post lights came on, turning the field bright as day.

He released her wrist and Kim sat down, defeated. What a rollercoaster night, from anger at Aunt Lang, to joy at rekindling a friendship, to fear at the trouble she was in. Unsure how to process so many emotions, Kim shut down, not moving or talking. Her body felt heavy as stone, but her heart was racing like an overheated engine.

Jayna's legs seemed to buckle as she sat down next to Kim. "Please let us go. My mom and dad will wonder where I am. I want to go home." Jayna's words came out in gasps like the puffs of steam coming from a train.

In the distance, Kim heard the loud wail of a siren. Her heart almost stopped when she realized the police were coming to the soccer field.

"I'm tired of staying up all night, just so I can catch you in the act," the man said. "This time, I called the police. Follow me."

The security guard led Jayna and Kim down the steps to the stadium entrance where a policeman waited. The policeman was short with a round stomach hanging over his dark pants. He took off his hat, showing a balding head with small brown tufts of hair around his ears.

The guard looked from the girls to the policeman. "Caught these two sneaking around here. Pretty sure they're the ones who broke in last week."

"I'm Officer McCleary," the policeman said as Jayna and Kim approached him. "What in the world are you doing here at midnight?"

Taking turns, Jayna and Kim explained how they ended up at the soccer field. Officer McCleary turned to the guard, "Bill, I don't think these are the vandals. They're just a couple of runaways."

The guard scowled. "They're trespassing and I want to press charges."

The policeman looked sympathetic. "All right. I'll take them off your hands." He wrote down their names and addresses. "Girls, come with me," he said, motioning toward his police car.

Kim regretted running out of her house. She wished she stayed and talked to Aunt Lang, but at the time, it seemed like putting space between them was the best thing to do. Jayna was quiet. They followed Officer McCleary. Kim felt like she was walking the gangplank on a pirate ship. When they reached the car, he opened the back door and motioned for them to get in. After settling into the driver's seat, he slammed his door, and slowly rumbled across the parking lot.

Kim and Jayna leaned their heads against the hard plastic seat. The muffled buzz of the radio broke the silence. Kim guessed they weren't enough of an emergency to turn on the siren, and she was glad for that. When they turned onto the road, another car slowly made its way toward them. Kim thought she recognized it. Could it be Aunt Lang's car? She quickly dismissed the idea, knowing that Lang never drove in the dark. She dropped her head to her chest. The night couldn't get any worse.

Beside her, Jayna shivered. "I'm scared. I've never gotten into trouble my entire life and now I've been arrested."

Kim looked at Jayna and her lips turned up in a slight smile. "Well, this might just get you out of playing soccer."

A half giggle, half groan escaped from Jayna's lips. Kim grasped Jayna's hand and whispered, "It'll be okay. They don't put kids in jail." She tried to sound more confident than she felt. Then she blinked to stop her tears. Crying wouldn't solve the problem and it would just make Jayna more upset, but it took everything she had to be brave.

32 ~ Are Pirates Real? 1977

After a warm, humid night, the sixth day at sea began with a blazing sun. The refugees spent their time wedged next to each other, barely moving. They were tired, hot, and thirsty. Lang slept most of the time and Tran played with a tiny wooden boat Duc whittled for him. The only thing that kept Mai going was hope.

The angry red streaks on Lang's leg disappeared and Mai noticed scabs forming where the bullet entered and exited. The medic stopped by to check the wounds, and he encouraged Lang to try walking. Shaking her head, she stayed in her spot, refusing to stand or move.

Duc stopped by frequently to talk to Mai, Lang and Tran. It was a bright spot in their long day, and Tran joyfully jumped up and down whenever he heard Duc's voice. He told them stories about his sea adventures and the countries he visited. While he talked, Mai studied Duc's animated face and muscular arms. She was grateful he kept them entertained and secretly wondered what might have been if they met under other circumstances.

"Good news," Duc said as he patted the top of Tran's head. "We should reach Indonesia tomorrow, a day ahead of schedule, if everything goes well."

Mai smiled. She knew they could put up with the heat and rationed water if it was only for another day. Duc turned to Tran, describing the lush green forests and sweet tropical fruits in Indonesia. He told a nonsensical story about a Komodo dragon who liked to greet the boats as they entered the harbor.

When Duc finished, he rose and looked into the horizon, as if searching for land. He glanced back at Mai, his mouth twisted and body tense. Mai stood and peered over the edge. A large speedboat was rapidly approaching. At least eight men, with colorful bandanas on their heads and rifles slung over their shoulders, stood on the deck.

Mai's forehead wrinkled in confusion. "Who are they?"

"Pirates," Duc ordered. "Get down."

Mai ducked. She heard that pirates patrolled the South China Sea looking for boats containing refugees with money and valuables, but she didn't believe it until now. It seemed more like a folktale or story in a children's book. The speedboat cut through the waves and the distance between them shortened. Duc ran to the helm and turned it sharply to the right, away from the approaching boat. With a flick of his hand, he turned up the throttle on the engine which made it squeal and rumble. His boat turned and moved in the opposite direction.

Mai yelled to Duc, "How can I help?"

Duc called back to her while focusing on driving. "I'm going to try to outrun them." Mai heard the lack of confidence in his shaky voice. "If they do come aboard, stay quiet. Hide if you can. If they ask for money, give it to them."

She looked around, trying to find somewhere they could hide. Mai grabbed two wooden boxes that once held supplies and ran back to Lang and Tran. She piled the boxes in front of them, one on top of the other. Then she ran back for more. They lay on their stomachs, heads resting on their arms. Even though the day was hot, Mai unfolded the blanket Lang used to prop her leg up and pulled it over their heads. Tran whimpered so she gently clamped a hand over his mouth to quiet him.

As Duc coaxed the boat to full speed, a blast of gunshots followed. She could feel Lang's body tense at each shotgun blast, and Mai grasped her hand to calm her. She shuddered at the thought of someone else being shot. Bullets rocketed over the hull and landed with a plop in the water on the other side. After a metallic clunk, the motor died and the boat lurched to a stop. The gunfire stopped and the churn of the motor from the pirates' boat became louder as it pulled beside theirs.

Mai peered out of the corner of the blanket and saw four men slide over the side of their boat, rifles in hand. The men wore loose black pants and sturdy boots. Three had bushy beards and long hair that touched their shoulders, while one, who looked like a teenager, had short, combed hair. They looked like regular men; not the pirates she read about in books.

Lowering her head, Mai left an opening in the blanket where she could peer around the side of the boxes. The pirates stopped in front of a young couple, demanding money and gold. They reluctantly reached into their pockets and handed over their valuables. Mai heard a man claim he didn't have any valuables and the pirates hit him with the butt of a gun. He cried out and then it grew quiet. She guessed people were handing over their jewelry and money. Mai's hand moved to her mother's necklace. It was tucked inside her tunic, the tall collar hiding the thin chain around her neck. Courage surged through her as she touched its smooth surface.

Twice, Mai heard screams and shots ring out. Tran whimpered and huge tears slid from his blue eyes to his sunburnt cheeks. Mai patted his back and then reached over to squeeze Lang's hand. Lang squeezed back, but didn't say a word. Mai couldn't believe that less than a week ago, she was sitting at the kitchen table, eating dinner with her family. How could life change that fast? She pulled the blanket around them right before the young pirate made his way toward the boxes they were hiding behind. They flattened themselves against the floor, and miraculously, Tran remained still. She heard the pirate kick the boxes and they toppled over. Mai took a deep breath in relief when the blanket wasn't pulled off them. The pirate must have moved on.

They cowered under the blanket, but could still hear the pounding of the pirate's feet on the deck. "I know you have more gold than that," one said.

"You have taken everything I own," a refugee rasped.

Soon after, there was a scream and a huge splash. Mai inhaled quickly to keep herself from crying out. She could hear someone flailing in the water, shouting for help. After a final gunshot blast, all was quiet for a few moments. Then the pirate ship's engine roared, churning the ocean water. Mai tentatively lifted the blanket and pulled it off when she was certain the pirates were gone. Someone threw a round life ring to the man who was thrown overboard and pulled him to the ladder. Another person pressed a cloth to an injured man's head.

Looking around, Mai was thankful everyone was safe. Most refugees sat quietly, and a few cried. Duc rushed to the helm to start the engine. There was a loud "Thawank" and then silence. He tried again and was met with the same sound before the engine died. Moving to the stern, he peered over and then looked back at the passengers. "A bullet hit the engine. We'll have to wait to be rescued."

Mai moved her hand to her chest, clutching the necklace hidden under her tunic. Family and Courage. She hoped it also meant Luck.

33 ~ Arrested?
2024

A feeling of doom hung heavy in the air. Kim could hear the static of the police radio over Jayna's muffled cries. At this time of night, in a small town, there wasn't much to hear on the radio.

Kim felt the police car slow down and round a corner. Officer McCleary turned down the radio and cleared his throat. "It seems like both of you have some problems that need to be worked out, but sneaking out and meeting up on a soccer field in the middle of the night isn't the best way to solve them."

Kim raised her head. Officer McCleary talked about the importance of family and dealing with problems instead of running away. "When I was about your age, my dad canceled our vacation to the Wisconsin Dells because he had to work. I was so disappointed, and mad, so I decided to go on vacation by myself. While my dad was sleeping, I stole his car. I could barely see out the windshield but managed to drive around town and onto the highway by sitting on a pillow."

Kim leaned forward so she could hear better. "What happened?"

Officer McCleary grinned. "Luckily, an observant police officer noticed the car speeding down the highway with my head barely above the steering wheel. When I saw the red lights flashing, I almost wet my pants. I pulled over, expecting to be arrested. He got in my car and drove me home, talking to me the whole way. From that day on, I decided to become a policeman."

Jayna and Kim looked at each other and asked the same question at the same time. "What did your parents do when you got home?"

Officer McCleary laughed. "Let's just say I didn't see friends or watch television for a long time. But that was still not as bad as getting arrested."

After turning another corner, the car stopped. They were parked in front of her house; not in front of the police station, as she expected. Officer McCleary got out and opened the back door. As Kim's eyes adjusted to the bright overhead light, she looked up at him. He looked more like somebody's kind father than a stern policeman.

Jayna leaned forward. "So, you aren't going to arrest us?"

"I think if I deliver you to your parents, it will make more of an impact."

Kim slid out and stood next to him, the pit in her stomach growing bigger. She pointed to Aunt Lang's house. "My parents are on vacation and I'm staying with my aunt. She lives next door." They walked toward her house, but it wasn't until they got to the front door that panic took over. Aunt Lang was already mad at Kim for snooping in the attic. She was sure that being woken up by a police officer returning her runaway niece would multiply that anger.

Kim pleaded with Officer McCleary. "I think that being arrested might be easier than having to deal with my angry aunt."

He looked sympathetic, but that didn't stop him from ringing the doorbell. Kim noticed all the lights in the house were on, but nobody came to the door. Worried, she pressed her index finger to the doorbell. The chimes sang a short song and then repeated over and over because Kim refused to take her finger off the doorbell.

Officer McCleary gently pulled her hand away. "She isn't home."

It hadn't occurred to Kim that Aunt Lang would be out looking for her. She didn't think Lang cared that much. "What do I do now?" Her voice was thin and quavering.

"I'll take Jayna home and then we come back."

They got back in the car just as a voice broke through the static on the radio. "Unit 65. We have a woman here who is looking for her niece. Please return to headquarters."

Kim slumped when she heard that Aunt Lang was at the station, waiting for her. How would Aunt Lang know to look for her at the police station? Kim was too scared to ask. "Now I'm really in trouble," she mumbled.

After responding to the dispatcher, Officer McCleary drove to Jayna's house. The house was flooded with lights, both inside and out. Kim watched as he walked her to the door and rang the doorbell. The door immediately opened, and Jayna's mom peered out. She pulled Jayna into her arms. "You're back. I'll call your dad. He's out looking for you."

Officer McCleary stepped inside for a few minutes. Returning to the car, he got in, radioed the dispatcher, and then drove back to the station. When they arrived, he opened the back door and Kim reluctantly got out of the police car and followed him in. "Where's Aunt Lang?"

Officer McCleary didn't answer, so she followed him down a long hallway, their hollow footsteps echoing off the walls. The black and beige tile floor was scratched and dirty. Peeling walls and a water-stained ceiling made the building look sad and gloomy. She blinked under the dull yellow lights.

Putting his hand on Kim's back, Officer McCleary guided her into a room. "Stay here and I'll find her." The small room held a dented metal desk and two chairs. He motioned to a chair. "Can I get you water or something to eat?"

Although Kim was hungry earlier, now her stomach felt like there was a rock sitting in it. She sat down in the rounded plastic chair. "No, thank you."

Officer McCleary left the room, closing the door behind him. Kim leaned forward, placing her elbows on her knees. She rested her head on her hands, wishing she could go back in time before she found the boxes.

Kim wasn't sure how long she waited before the door opened again. Officer McCleary walked in, followed by Aunt Lang. She was wearing her old blue cotton jacket with a matching silk scarf tied under her neck. Her bad leg dragged behind her, making a scraping noise at each step. Kim's heartbeat quickened. She knew Lang only pulled her leg behind her when she was very tired.

Lang enveloped Kim in her arms. "I was so worried."

Kim wrapped her arms around Lang. "I'm sorry. Have you been out searching for me all night?"

Lang dropped her arms and lowered herself into the chair next to Kim's. "At first, I thought you would be back home within an hour so I just stayed put. While I waited, I looked through that old scrapbook."

Kim hung her head. She knew the scrapbook brought back sad memories.

"When you didn't come back, I checked your house, but you weren't there. I got worried and went out looking for you." She told Kim about walking through downtown, looking for her in every restaurant and open store.

"Around midnight, I panicked. I was just about to call the police when I remembered your mom telling me you always go to the soccer field when you are worried or sad. Before calling the police, I thought I'd try there."

Lang looked so tired. She grimaced and shifted in the chair to get comfortable. Kim felt guilty. What kind of person was she to not even think about the worry she put Lang through? "But I was at the soccer field and didn't see you," Kim said.

Lang reached out, her icy fingers resting on Kim's hand. "My leg was aching, so I went back home to get my car, and drove to the soccer field. As I pulled into the parking lot, a police car pulled out. Thinking you might be in the car, I turned around and drove to the police station."

The tears Kim was holding in all night finally trickled down her face. "That must have been your car we passed when we left the stadium. I should have said something when I saw you, but I was so scared. Oh, Aunt Lang, I just want to go home."

Officer McCleary spoke up. "I need to write up a report, but as far as I'm concerned, you can go home with your aunt."

Kim pulled herself out of the chair. "Officer McCleary, thank you. For everything." She helped Aunt Lang up and they headed for the door before he changed his mind.

34 ~ Typhoon Fury 1977

Three days passed since the pirate attack, and to Mai, who spent hours looking out at the ocean, a rescue seemed hopeless. The boat floated aimlessly, a tiny dot on an endless sea, waiting to be noticed by another ship. The day before, Duc started rationing food, a sign that he also didn't have much faith in being rescued. Adding to the gloom was Lang's attempts at walking. She could only take a few steps before her leg gave out.

That night, the sky was littered with dark gray, pink, and black streaks. Tiny clouds grew larger, as if the raging wind was blowing them up like balloons. Tran, Lang, and Mai covered themselves with their scratchy blanket and huddled near the bow. The waves grew larger, and the boat tossed up and down. After surviving a pirate attack, facing a storm seemed like more than they could handle. Trying to calm the panic that was squeezing her from the inside out, Mai sang silly songs to Tran. He clapped his hands and giggled, oblivious to the storm. Lang looked at Mai and frowned.

As the night darkened, cool raindrops grew bigger and more frequent, and the wind gusted. Waves pushed toward the boat, toppling over the sides in a waterfall. Duc was at the helm, trying to guide the boat, the wheel twisting and turning in his hand like an angry serpent. "We need to get the water out of the boat. Grab buckets or whatever you can find, and bail."

Mai grabbed a bucket and dumped out the fishing supplies. She scooped up the water streaming down the deck and threw it overboard. Tran grabbed a cup and filled it with water, but he was too small to toss it overboard. Each wave was like a mountain the wooden boat struggled to climb. Before it reached the crest, the next wave crashed against its side, sending more water over the deck. Over and over, the boat plunged up and down.

In school, Mai read about typhoons, but she never imagined being in one. The rain came down in an endless stream and roaring thunder drowned out Mai's calls to Lang for help. Although the refugees bailed, more water came in than went out. Mai took a short break to rest her arms and check on Lang and Tran. With the fury of the storm fighting against her, Lang pulled herself to standing and then collapsed onto the deck. Mai saw Lang struggling. She wanted to help her, but knew getting water out of the boat was more pressing.

Thunder exploded and lightning flashed across the sky in a spectacular show of fireworks. The rain came down like sharp daggers. While she bailed, Mai looked at Lang who sat in a puddle of water. Her hands were wrapped around her injured leg like a bandage. Tran sat and placed his tiny hands on top of hers. Lang raised her arms and pushed Tran away. He turned toward Mai, his wails drowned out by the howling wind.

Mai dropped her bucket, and it clattered against the side of the boat before landing. Gathering Tran in her arms, she held him tightly until his cries softened. She set him down on a box next to Lang, anger building in her like a storm. "Lang, you need to watch Tran. I don't care how much your leg hurts. Step up and help out."

Lang turned her back to them. Mai covered Tran with the blanket before returning to bailing. Her arms felt heavy as she scooped water. Her shoulders and hands were cramping. She looked around, noticing many refugees' motions were slower and some were resting. The look of defeat on them gave Mai a burst of energy, making her bail faster and harder.

The typhoon continued to bear down, a wild horse caught in a pen, and the boat listed to one side. "Move to the other side," Duc yelled.

People grasped hands, helping each other move. Mothers grabbed their children by their clothing and pulled them to the other side. Their panicked cries were partially drowned by the waves as they crashed against the boat. Lang managed to crawl to the other side by grasping a rope dangling from the side while Mai pulled Tran behind her by his collar. The boat groaned and uprighted itself. Thunder echoed, lightning flickered in the dark sky, and the refugees returned to bailing water.

Just as fast as the storm began, it ended. The thunder grew softer and the lightning streaks turned to dim lines, occasionally breaking through the dark sky. Raindrops became a light mist and then ended altogether. The smell of seaweed and dead fish hung in the air. The boat aimlessly bobbed in the waves, heading west and then slowly turning east as the refugees continued to bail water.

The remaining water drained from the boat through a scupper hole at the bow. Duc stood in the middle of the boat, waving to get the attention of the refugees. They stood with arms wrapped around their family, faces haggard and clothes drenched. His voice was raspy as he talked. "We survived. Let's get some sleep and assess the damage to the boat in the morning."

The deck was still wet, but Mai was so tired, she didn't care. The thunderstorm ended, but a storm of emotions still raged in her. She sat down next to Tran and Lang. Tran must have forgiven Lang because his head rested on her shoulder. She shivered as the breeze worked on drying their dripping clothes.

Lang looked at Mai. "I'm never going to walk again. It's too hard," she said dully. Her brown eyes were lifeless, and she curled into a ball, like a turtle retreating into its shell.

"You don't know that. Your leg is still healing. When we get to Indonesia, you will grow stronger, and you can practice walking on firm ground instead of a shaky boat." Mai didn't know if she believed her own words, but she wanted to give Lang hope.

"I really wanted this to work, to live in the United States and play soccer on a real team, but I know I'll never play again. My dreams are shattered." Lang's expression turned stormy and she gritted her teeth. "I hate the Vietnamese soldiers who forced us to leave. I hate this broken boat. And I hate you for making promises you can't keep."

The venom in her voice shocked Mai. Should Lang have stayed in Vietnam with her parents? Was this trip a big mistake? Without soccer, Mai knew Lang was right when she said her dreams were shattered, but Lang had to know there was no future in Vietnam. Lang turned her back to Mai, the silence like a thick wall between them. She slept fitfully, her arms and legs thrashing like a prisoner caught in chains. Mai remained awake, angry at Lang, hating herself, and questioning if she made the right decision.

As the sky cleared and a few stars peeked out, Mai's mind cleared. The government took their pharmacy and home. Her parents would work low-paying jobs or beg for food. Soldiers could jail adults and break families apart without reason. She knew she made the right decision. No matter what happened, they couldn't go back and it wasn't fair that Lang blamed her. Mai finally fell asleep.

When dawn broke, Mai stood up to stretch. Her clothes were still damp from the typhoon and her shoulders burned. Pushing herself to move, she gripped the edge of the boat and peered out. Where the sky met the ocean, it was crimson red and lilac purple. A pale yellow mound—the very top of the sun—broke through the deep colors. It was a spectacular sight. Then Mai looked south and was amazed to see a mass of land in the distance. Their boat lazily drifted towards it.

A few other people were up and chattered excitedly when they saw land. Mai saw Duc stretched out on the floor of the boat, just below the helm. She walked over and nudged his shoulder. "Duc. Wake up!" He raised his head. Mai grinned and pointed toward the land.

35 ~ Sharing Secrets 2024

The drive home was short in distance but felt like it took forever. Lang drove, hands gripping the steering wheel and staring straight ahead. Kim sat in the front passenger seat, body tense and looking ahead as well. Whether it was exhaustion or being unsure of what to say, neither of them talked.

Lang finally broke the silence. "So, did you run away because of the trouble with your team?"

Kim's shoulders slumped. "Partly. I feel like my whole team is against me. And I miss Mom and Dad. I've never been away from them for this long. But mostly, I ran away because of you. You shut me out and treat me like a stranger instead of family. I don't get it."

They pulled into the driveway and Lang opened her mouth, but no words came out. She snapped her mouth shut, took the key out of the ignition, and exited the car. Kim got out and followed her into the house. Inside, Lang shrugged off her jacket and wrapped a soft pink shawl around her hunched shoulders while Kim stood awkwardly, not sure what to do. Lang beckoned Kim to the kitchen. "I know it's late, but I have too many thoughts in my head to sleep."

Kim followed. "I should be tired too, but I'm not." The scrapbooks, newspaper clippings, and ribbons attached to colorful strings were strewn over the table. A chair was askew, as if Lang had been sitting at the table earlier, looking through the items.

Lang pointed to an empty chair at the end of the table. "Sit."

After sitting, Kim studied Lang's face. Her eyes were red rimmed and swollen. Puffy dark half-moons sat below them like shadowy reflections in a pool. Had Aunt Lang been crying? Because Kim ran away or because she was sad about the things spread out on the table?

Lang took two cups out of the cupboard and placed a spoon in each one. Kim knew what that meant. Lang must have something important she wanted to say. She always made tea when the adults in the family had important discussions.

While Lang waited for the water to boil, she turned to Kim. "You figured out that I used to play soccer, or as we called it, football, in Vietnam. My team was just a ragtag group of boys and girls who were looking for something to take our minds off the war. But I fell in love with soccer and dreamed of playing it in college in the United States."

Lang put the tea bags in the cups, along with a cinnamon stick and jasmine leaf like she always did, while Kim watched. "Did you play college soccer?" Kim asked.

The room was quiet, except for the soft click of the spoon against the cup while Lang stirred the tea. She shuffled over, carrying the cups and set them down, wearily lowering herself into the chair next to Kim. "No. I didn't, and that is why I got so angry when you found my box. I didn't want to be reminded—"

"I'm sorry, Aunt Lang," Kim interrupted. She felt hot tears gathering on her bottom lids. "I'm sorry that I snooped in your boxes."

Lang held up her hand like a stop sign. Her voice was firm and filled the kitchen. "There have been too many secrets hidden away like those boxes in the attic. It's time for the secrets to end. Hmmm … where to begin?"

Lang's lips turned up in a soft smile and her hands fluttered while she looked for something on the table. Finally, she found it. She picked up a yellowed newspaper clipping that contained the picture of a young man in a military jacket and cap. The headline, written in Vietnamese, was in large blocky letters. With a solemn expression, Lang turned the article toward her, translating the headline from Vietnamese to English as she read it.

Soldier Killed By Escaping Refugee

"I don't understand," Kim said. "What does this have to do with you?"

Lang put her finger to her lips to silence Kim and read the whole article out loud. The article talked about how a refugee on a fishing boat leaving from Vung Tau Beach shot a Vietnamese soldier before the boat got away. Aunt Lang set the article on the table. "We were on that boat. That soldier shot me."

Kim gasped. "Did you or Grandma Mai kill that soldier?"

Lang scowled. "No. But someone on our boat did. I never wanted to know." Then she launched into the story of the day they escaped from Vietnam years ago.

Kim shuddered while listening to Lang recount that awful day. Every once in a while, Lang's voice trembled, and she had to stop for a few minutes before continuing. She brushed tears away often, smiled when she talked about them wading into the water with high hopes of being in the United States in a few days, and broke down when she talked about being shot.

"I didn't want Mai to go to Vietnam because it would stir up too many bad memories. Things I tried to forget."

So many questions swirled in Kim's head. She thought Grandma Mai and Aunt Lang came to America on an airplane directly from Vietnam because they wanted to open a business. She thought that Lang limped from being in an accident. And she never thought about the family they left behind.

Why hadn't she asked more questions? What happened to Grandma's parents? Why didn't Grandma Mai ever talk about why she left Vietnam? How did Grandma Mai and Aunt Lang finally get to America? Kim was ashamed. "I was so busy living my life that I never asked about yours."

"It was a relief you didn't ask. We weren't ready to talk about it," Lang said.

"Do Mom and Dad know the story about your awful boat escape from Vietnam?"

Lang nodded. "When your dad was younger, we never talked about Vietnam. He used to ask questions, but when we avoided answering he stopped. After Mai's health scare, she decided it was time to share our story with your dad and return to Vietnam. I was against it."

"Why? It happened so long ago," Kim said.

"It is hard for me to talk about. Decisions I made back then changed my life. I live with regret every day."

Kim saw the sadness in Aunt Lang's eyes. She didn't want to upset Lang more by asking about those decisions. "I'm sorry you're so sad. When something bad happens to me, Dad always tells me, *'You can't change the direction of the wind, but you can adjust your sail.'* Maybe it isn't too late for you to adjust your sail. To make a change in your life."

"Maybe." Aunt Lang seemed to be lost in her own thoughts. She glanced at the clock on the wall. "It's late and we're both tired. We can talk more in the morning." She yawned and got up. "One more thing. After you ran away, your parents called. They could tell something was wrong and insisted they talk to you, so I had to tell them you ran away. Their plane leaves in a few hours. They're coming home."

Surprisingly, Kim felt a surge of relief instead of dread that she was in trouble. She hugged Aunt Lang. Her parents were exactly what she needed now.

36 ~ Telling the Truth 1977

Mai smiled at Duc. "Is that Indonesia?" Smooth narrow tree trunks topped by mounds of pointy leaves swayed in the breeze. Wide, wispy ferns poked from the ground beneath the trees.

Duc stood up and peered over the edge. He grinned. "Look at those tall trees. Those are a special kind of teak tree you only find in Indonesia." The towering trees crowded the sandy shore. Mai saw several men pushing through the ferns and trees to make their way to the beach.

Duc and another man dropped a massive anchor over the side of the boat, and it came to a gentle stop fifty meters from shore. The lack of motion awakened the rest of the refugees who looked over the side and broke into cheers. Mai hurried over to Lang and Tran, beaming with excitement. They would soon be on their way to America. Lifting Tran, they gazed at the mounds of green vegetation. Mai tried to explain to Tran what was happening. He didn't understand, but he shouted and clapped like the other refugees.

"Look," Mai shouted to Lang who still sat on the deck, wearing a sullen expression. Mai put Tran down and grabbed Lang's arms to help her up. For a twelve-year old, Lang was slim and strong, so Mai expected to pull her up easily. Instead, Lang lashed out, pushing Mai so hard that she tumbled back against the wall of the boat. She gasped when she landed with a thud.

"Leave me alone," Lang snapped. "I have no reason to go to the United States now. I can barely walk. My life is ruined."

Mai lost her temper. She pulled herself off the ground and angrily grabbed both of Lang's arms. "Get up." This wasn't the time to feel sorry for Lang. Life was different now, and Lang would have to grow up. Taking a deep, calming breath, Mai tried to give Lang hope. "I truly believe you will recover and play soccer again."

Lang pulled her arms away from Mai and scooched back by pushing her legs against the deck. "Leave me alone. You don't understand," Lang seethed.

Mai stared at Lang and grinned.

"You're crazy," Lang said. "Why are you smiling?"

Mai's grin widened. "You used your injured leg to move across the deck. See, it is getting stronger."

Mai grabbed Lang under her arms and pulled her up. Lang gripped the side to steady herself as the boat bobbed in the choppy water. Duc picked up a long wooden stick he used when fishing and gently tucked it under Lang's arm like a crutch. She took a step, placing all her weight on the stick while Mai gripped her other arm. She leaned over since the stick was a bit short, but it seemed to work. Grimacing, Lang took another step.

The refugees moved toward the front of the boat, waiting to finally leave. When Mai saw they would have to wade through water to reach the shore, she was dizzy with anxiety. Lang could barely walk on flat ground. How would she manage in the water? Sighing, Mai picked up Tran and extended her arm for Lang to hold onto. In front of them was a long ramp that workers on the island brought to the side of the boat. Lang groaned. Holding the stick crutch with one arm and Mai with the other, she limped down the ramp.

Duc was waiting at the bottom. He smiled at Mai and gave her a quick hug. Duc picked up Lang and carried her to shore while Mai walked through the water holding Tran. When he gently set Lang down. Mai's eye's caught Duc's. "Thank you."

He took her hand. "I'd like to think that in another time, we would have been more than friends. For now, I need to repair my boat and return to Vietnam as soon as possible. Good luck on your journey, Mai." Mai's heart ached. Before she could respond, Duc stepped back into the water and returned to the boat.

A short, stocky military officer, wearing a wrinkled white shirt, dark pants and a wide belt, waited for the refugees to gather around him. His round face, full red lips and tufts of dark hair sticking out in all directions made him look clown-like, but his expression was serious.

"Welcome to Indonesia," he said. "We are glad you arrived safely. Our government will immediately begin working on getting approvals to send you to your destination. In the meantime, I am Kevin, and I will be escorting you to Galang Camp, the refugee village. Follow me."

Kevin guided the parade of refugees down a dirt path in the woods. The morning was hot, and the air heavy with the scent of hibiscus. Mai and Tran fell behind so they could help Lang whose face beaded with sweat. After several minutes of walking, Lang lowered herself onto a log. "I can't go on," she cried, rubbing her leg.

Mai wanted to let Lang rest, but knew they couldn't stop. Worried Kevin would send them back if he saw that Lang was injured, Mai pulled her up. She didn't want Lang to know that being sent back was an option. "Keep moving. You can do it." To Mai's relief, two refugees who lagged behind them caught up. Each positioned an arm under Lang's and supported her as she walked.

Mai turned around to pick up Tran who was walking slower and slower. The edges of her lips turned up into a small smile when she watched Lang gingerly making her way down the path. Sometimes struggle makes you stronger, Mai thought. Lang turned her head back and glared at Mai with hatred, and her smile faded.

Ten minutes later, they walked into a clearing surrounded by a tall wood fence lashed together with vines. A long building sat on a dusty field, surrounded by several other small buildings. Hundreds of Vietnamese refugees gathered in small groups, talking or listlessly sitting in the sun. Little kids ran in the field, kicking a partially deflated ball. Mai had the sinking feeling they wouldn't be boarding a plane today.

"You will sleep in the bunkhouse," Kevin shouted, waving an arm at the long building. "During the day, you will be assigned jobs and take classes to learn English. For now, follow me to the Resettlement office where you can register."

Mai turned to an older man who often helped Duc on the boat. "I don't understand. I thought we would be boarding a plane to the United States today or tomorrow." The change in plans made her so nervous her stomach hurt.

"No. That is how it used to be. Now, there are too many refugees for countries to handle at one time. You must have a sponsor before leaving the camp," he said.

Disappointed, Mai had to work to form her next question. "How ... um ... how long will that take?"

The man shrugged. "Weeks, months, maybe years."

Mai was so shocked that she took a step back and almost fell. Why didn't she know that? She realized just how unprepared they were for their journey. Wondering what other surprises awaited left her head foggy and body shaky.

Several hours later, Mai was called into the Resettlement office. She hoped Lang was able to handle Tran. He was an energetic toddler and Lang couldn't chase after him. A tall man with a shaggy black beard stepped away from the doorway, and Mai walked in. The room was empty except for a battered wooden desk brimming with papers. A row of offices lined the side. An Indonesian soldier and a dark-haired woman sat behind the desk.

"Give me your papers," the soldier said, his voice edged with irritation. It wasn't until now she remembered their travel documents were in the backpack that sunk to the bottom of the sea during their escape. Mai saw wavy lines and her head spun. She leaned on the desk. Could they be sent back after all their work to escape Vietnam?

The woman filled a paper cup with water from a dented thermos and brought it to Mai. "Are you okay?"

Mai lowered herself onto a bench and took slow sips from the cup. The wavy lines began to disappear. She looked up at the woman. "I don't have any papers. Please don't send us back." She told the woman about their desperate escape while being shot at. The soldier remained behind the desk, a frown etched between his saggy cheeks. The woman smiled and patted Mai's shoulder before returning to her desk.

"Let's start by filling out the forms requesting duplicate paperwork from Vietnam and permission to enter the United States. Are there other family members with you?"

Mai gulped. Tran wasn't a family member and she wasn't sure how to explain him, so she made a quick decision. "My sister is with me and I have a son. His name is Tran. He's three and he is Amerasian."

The woman nodded and took out another form. "Let me guess. You had this child at home and the father was shipped out, leaving you behind."

Mai nodded, embarrassed but not quite understanding why. After handing a pen to Mai, the woman slid the papers toward Mai. "Your sister will need documentation, but because your son is Amerasian, the United States does not require papers for him."

Mai relaxed, feeling a surge of gratefulness when she realized the woman would help her. "How long will it take before we go to America?"

"You're in luck. Often, it takes more than a year, but the United States speeds up the process when an Amerasian child is involved," she said. "It may only take a few months. Until then, you'll stay at Galang."

Encouraged, Mai filled out the forms before leaving to find Lang. She knew bringing Tran with them was the right decision, and now he seemed like a lucky charm.

37 ~ Telling the Truth
2024

The next morning, Kim woke to her phone buzzing. The sun was already high, and the beams reaching through the window warmed her room. Rolling over in bed, she grabbed her phone and tapped Answer.

"It's me, Jayna."

Kim groaned. "I was sleeping. If you don't remember, we were up really, really late."

Jayna ignored Kim's groans. "I have great news and I want you to be the first to hear."

Kim could almost see Jayna smiling through the phone. She expected to hear from a sad, despondent, grounded Jayna. Not a happy Jayna. She kicked off the blankets and sat up. "So, you aren't grounded for life?"

"Oh, I'm grounded, all right, but I don't even care. I'm quitting soccer and taking art classes instead. Mom and Dad were mad when Officer McCleary brought me home, but they were relieved I was back."

In a rush of words, Jayna described the conversation with her parents. "This time, they really listened to all my reasons why I don't want to play soccer. They said they were sorry I had to run away to get them to listen."

Kim let out a whoop of joy. "What about your grandpa?"

"My parents said they would talk to him and tell him that playing soccer is my decision," Jayna said.

Surprisingly, Mai felt sad that Jayna would be leaving the team. They could have been teammates and friends like before. There was a brief silence. Then she heard Jayna sniffling. Was she crying? Kim waited for Jayna to explain why she was crying after getting such good news.

"I still feel awful that I was so mean to you," Jayna said. "I can't believe all the stuff I did to you. Every time my grandfather pointed out how good you are, I got more and more jealous."

Kim moved the phone away from her ear so Jayna's words were softer. She couldn't explain it, but the apology annoyed her slightly. "You were mean. After everything, I'm still thinking about quitting," she said honestly. Kim knew that her words stung Jayna because her sobs were louder.

"I'm sorry," Jayna said. "I hope you won't quit. I wish I could make things better."

Kim wasn't sure if things would ever get better on the team, even if Jayna wasn't there. A new bully might take Jayna's place. "I'll have to think about it. Mom and Dad are coming home today, so I want to talk to them."

Kim wasn't sure what else there was to say and Jayna was quiet too. It would take some time to figure things out, but she knew she and Jayna forged a bond over their crazy night.

Jayna broke the silence. "Friends?"

Kim smiled. "Friends."

After ending the call, Kim went downstairs. Lang was sitting on the couch, knitting, as if nothing had happened the night before. "Aunt Lang, I want to know more about your life. I have so many questions. About you and Grandma Mai."

Lang kept knitting. The silence caused anxiety to grip Kim, making her feel like she was being squeezed between two black walls. Lang was always angry, so Kim expected her to respond with anger. She shuddered, waiting for the sharp words.

Lang blinked, as if coming out of a daze, and put down her knitting. "Come with me. I have more to tell you." She limped to the kitchen.

Lang's limp was worse. Kim could almost feel the pain when she looked at the grimace on Aunt Lang's face. Lang pushed a big scrapbook closer to Kim, who stood on the other side of the table. "A few years after we settled in America, my parents shipped a box containing this scrapbook and the ribbons to me." Lang's long index finger tapped the top of the scrapbook.

"When I first opened the box and saw what was in there, I was so angry. I didn't want to think about what could have been. I slammed the lid down and never opened it again. I thought Mai got rid of this box years ago."

Lang leaned against the table and closed her eyes, as if that would shut out the memories. Kim pulled the scrapbook in front of her. It was a deep red with a gold diamond pattern across the cover. She opened the cover of the scrapbook. The first page contained a picture of a smiling, brown-eyed little girl clutching a soccer ball. "Is that you, Aunt Lang?"

Lang looked at the picture and smiled. "I think I was about seven in that picture. It was when I first discovered football, what you kids call soccer, and fell in love."

"That's how old I was when I fell in love with soccer," Kim said. She was beginning to understand that she and Aunt Lang had a lot in common.

"The war was still going on. Football took our mind off the war, but there wasn't any money for real teams like you are on. Back then, in Vietnam, girls usually didn't play sports." Lang told Kim about her coach, a former professional football player, who put teams of boys and girls together to play for fun.

Kim's attention returned to the scrapbook, and they sat next to each other at the table. Sometimes, she asked Lang to read a newspaper clipping, and sometimes, she just examined the photos. As Lang gazed at the scrapbook, she launched into stories about her teammates, an exciting game, or a football hero mentioned in the newspaper articles. Lang smiled as Kim turned each page.

When they finished looking through the entire scrapbook, Kim closed the cover. "Aunt Lang, I bet you were very good, but you never told me you played soccer in Vietnam."

Lang drew in a breath. "I had such big dreams when I was your age. Although most of Asia had professional women's soccer teams, Vietnam did not. They were still recovering from the war. I wanted to move to the United States where I could play professional soccer when I got older."

Kim was confused. "So, why didn't you play?"

Lang shrugged. "Something didn't heal right in my leg. It was stiff and painful. Doctors told me with physical therapy, I could play soccer again, but I was too angry to believe them. Instead, I just gave up on my dreams."

Kim looked at Lang in dismay. "You just gave up? You didn't even try?"

Lang's mouth puckered and shiny tears caught in her eyelashes. "Moving to a new country. Learning a new language and customs. It was so hard. Kids teased me about my accent and strange lunches. I just didn't have the energy to devote to rehabilitating my leg and we didn't have the money to pay for physical therapy anyway. Yes. I gave up and I will always regret it. My life would have been so different. Now do you understand why I don't want you to just give up and quit soccer?"

Kim was grasping a soccer ribbon in each hand. They meant more than any medal or trophy she ever won. "I do."

38 ~ Visit From an Old Friend 1978

Over days, weeks and months, Mai settled into a routine at the camp. She and Lang accepted they would need to wait for new paperwork before they could travel to America. Most days went by quickly, but time crawled when she thought about how long it might be before they could leave.

Mai and Lang were assigned a narrow bed in the corner of a wooden bunkhouse with a tarpaulin roof. Tran slept curled up between them. Mai worked in the kitchen, preparing breakfast and lunch. Lang was assigned to the childcare unit where she cared for Tran and other refugee children while their parents worked. In the afternoon, they attended English class.

On a warm day, three months after arriving in Indonesia, Mai perched on a wooden log, peeling the skin from a spiny durian fruit. She was going to use it in a fruit salad for lunch. Mosquitos buzzed around her ears while she worked.

"Mai? Is that you?" The voice was deep and familiar.

Mai looked up and grinned. "Duc!" She stood up and gave him a hug. "I didn't think I'd ever see you again."

"I've been busy. During the day my uncle and I fish. We are making a good living, but I arrived today with another group of refugees. I had a feeling you would still be here." Duc sat down beside Mai. "I saw Lang and Tran. Lang ducked inside a building and wouldn't talk to me, but Tran was so excited."

Mai's smile flattened. "Her leg hurts all the time. She is angry we are here and she blames me. They asked her to teach the children how to play football, but she refused. The only time Lang seems happy is when she's working with the toddlers in the childcare center. I'm hoping she'll be happier when we get to America."

Duc reached into his jacket and pulled out a bulky envelope. "When I returned to Vietnam after leaving you, I wanted to do something to help. You told me your parents owned a pharmacy in Ho Chi Minh, so I looked for them." He handed her the envelope. "They sent this for you."

Astounded, Mai took the envelope. The first thing she pulled out was a letter. She teared up as she read. "Ba and Ma closed the store, but they still have their apartment above it. They are well. Ba said it is good we left Vietnam when we did."

Duc nodded. "Things are not the same there. Poverty and hunger is everywhere. At least your parents still have their home. Many people are living on the streets."

"Every day, I ask myself whether I made the right decision. Every day, Lang tells me we made a mistake by leaving. I finally feel like I did the right thing," Mai said. "Did you tell them about Lang's leg or Tran?"

Duc shook his head. "I didn't. I only told them that you are safe and waiting to go to the United States. Your parents asked me to visit them when I return."

"Thank you. I don't want them to know yet. They would worry about Lang and think I was crazy to take Tran." Mai looked in the envelope and pulled out a packet of documents paperclipped together. Slowly, she sifted through the papers. "These are our identification papers. It is what we need to travel to America. How—"

"You had nothing when you boarded. Without those papers, I knew your trip to the United States would be delayed. I told your parents about losing your backpack, hoping they might have copies of your identification papers."

Mai looked at the papers and then at Duc. "We can go to America."

Duc's smile reflected Mai's joy. He looked at her and his cheeks reddened. "I brought you this," he said, handing Mai a small leather journal and pen. "Use it to write about your journey. Someday, your children and grandchildren will want to know about it."

Mai opened the journal and leafed through the thin lined pages. Writing would give her something to do during the long evenings. She was touched that Duc still thought about her. "Thank you. I'll start with writing about you and our trip here. First, can you get a note back to my parents?"

Duc nodded and Mai hastily ripped a page out of the back of the journal. She uncapped the pen and wrote a short note telling her parents they were safe and looking forward to traveling to the United States soon. She folded the note and handed it to Duc.

Mai and Duc talked about his latest boat trip, the new refugees, and her life at camp. Duc's smile was gentle, but then it faded. "Mai, I'm happy for you, but I'm sad we can't be together. I think about you often." He bent his head and kissed her forehead.

Mai took Duc's hand in hers. "Yes, in different times."

39 ~ Quitting is an Option 2024

Holding onto a ribbon, Kim studied the picture of a soccer ball and the number 1 drawn on it. "I get that you don't want me to quit soccer since you regret quitting, but I have a good reason. It has nothing to do with being injured. You don't know what it's like to be hated by people you thought were your friends."

"We have more in common than you think," Lang said. "I was taunted because I was part of an ethnic group called the Hoa. Soldiers on the street blocked my way when I walked to the park to play football. Kids at the park called me names. They pushed and shoved when the coach wasn't looking. Jayna would have fit in very well on my football team."

Kim was surprised. So Aunt Lang put up with a bully, just like her? Was that one of the reasons why Grandma and Aunt Lang escaped from Vietnam? In a way, she was being forced to leave her team just like Aunt Lang was forced to leave hers. "Aunt Lang, I think you would understand after being bullied yourself. Why shouldn't I give up? You didn't want to be on a team like that and I don't want to either."

Aunt Lang's fist slammed against the table. Kim was startled to see the fury in her eyes. "You are wrong. In Vietnam, I wanted to play soccer so much that I avoided the soldiers and ignored the kids on my team. The bullies weren't going to stop me. I left Vietnam for the opportunity to play soccer and for a better life. I didn't quit because of bullying." Lang took a breath. "Having an injured leg was an excuse to quit. You have no excuse."

Kim felt sad for Lang and a little embarrassed complaining about problems that were so small compared to Lang's. After looking around for something and not finding it, Lang limped out of the room and up the stairs. A few minutes later she returned with the other box that Kim retrieved from the attic. Lang dumped the contents of the box on the table and sat down across from Kim. Envelopes littered the table.

"Months after arriving in the United States, Mai wrote to our father in Vietnam, explaining that I gave up on playing soccer. He tried to convince me to play, but it didn't work. It made me even angrier. I hope I am more persuasive than my father."

Lang spread out the envelopes until she found a light blue one. She pulled out a cream colored piece of paper and translated as she read.

Dear Mai and Lang,

Ma and I miss you so much. We are proud of you for beginning your new lives in the United States. I know how hard it must be, but we believe with our heart you will have much success. One day, Mai, you will open your own store instead of working for someone else.

Lang, Mai wrote to us that you refuse to rehabilitate your leg and don't want to play football. Please don't give up. In Vietnam, you kept going even when your teammates treated you so poorly. Your football team in Vietnam was disbanded, but in the United States, you have a second chance. Keep fighting!

We will send your ribbons and scrapbook when we can afford it. We hope those good memories will encourage you to return to playing. Don't let your injury become an excuse.

Ho Chi Minh is no longer safe, so we moved to the countryside near your aunt and uncle. Our new address is below. Your ma's heart is still too weak to travel, but our dream is to someday be with you in the United States. Until then, we are happy and safe in our new home. We love you and miss you.

Ba and Ma

Lang waved the letter in the air. "When I read this, it made me angry. I felt like nobody understood me, so I refused to open any more of my parents' letters. It wasn't until I was older and time softened my anger that I finally read them."

Kim felt sad that Aunt Lang's life was so difficult when she was young. Lang's parents weren't even around when she was injured or to help her adjust to the move. But that was a long time ago. "You still seem angry," Kim said.

Lang nodded. "For a long time, I didn't think about playing soccer. It wasn't until you started to play that the rage returned so deeply, it burned in my soul. You got to play soccer, and I foolishly threw away my chance to play. Don't waste your chance because of a bully."

40 ~ Discouraging News 1978

After Mai delivered the identification documents to the Indonesian government office, she met Tran and Lang who were walking to the bunkhouse.

Tran leaped into Mai's arms, giving her a tight squeeze. "Ma, Lang played a game with me today." After arriving at the camp, Tran took his cue from other kids and began calling her Ma. Mai was enchanted by Tran and her heart swelled every time he called her that. Tran's short life was filled with sorrow, and she was amazed he was so resilient.

"You are lucky that Lang takes such good care of you," Mai said as she ran her fingers through his straight black hair. It surprised her to see the softer side of Lang.

"I'm exhausted," Lang complained. "Those kids keep me busy all day and my leg aches. Every day, all I do is work." Lang no longer used the crutch, but she still limped. Before boarding the boat, Lang was a kid with a dream, but now, she was bitter. Mai noticed that, almost overnight, Lang changed from a young girl to a grumpy old woman.

Tran interrupted. "Duc was here today. He ate lunch with me."

Mai smiled. "I saw him. He brought good news. Lang, your daycare duties might be ending soon."

Lang leaned against the side of a weathered building and rubbed her injured leg. "What do you mean?"

"Duc found Ba and Ma. He brought identification papers for us. We may be leaving here soon," Mai said.

Lang's face softened. "I can't believe he did that for us, and I suppose the United States will be an improvement over Galang."

Mai hoped Lang would be more excited, but she was content that Lang still wanted to go to the United States. Mai twirled around, her braid swaying from side to side. "When our boat arrived in Indonesia, I told Duc the name of our store in Ho Chi Minh and asked him to get a message to Ma and Ba, telling them we were safe. I never expected him to return to Indonesia with our papers."

Lang asked Mai questions about Ma and Ba and smiled when she heard they still had their apartment. She moved to a nearby bench and sat down, her injured leg stretched out in front of her. "I've listened to some of the stories about Vietnam. My friend, Cam, was homeless before she escaped, and Chau's family left when they were arrested and sent to a reeducation camp. I know we can't go back there."

That night, while Tran slept, Lang and Mai talked about their plans. "I'm hoping I can find work in a pharmacy or other store," Mai said. She didn't want to worry Lang, but Mai wondered how she would support three people. She was grateful she turned eighteen, a legal adult, when they celebrated *Tết* while in Indonesia.

Lang stroked Tran's head while she listened to Mai's plans. "I'm not good at speaking English. I hope it won't be too difficult to understand my teachers."

Mai nodded. "I'm scared too. It's hard to move to a place so different and far away, but I can't wait." Believing they would leave soon, both were too excited to sleep.

A week later, a soldier was waiting outside the bunkhouse when Mai, Lang, and Tran emerged in the morning. "Are you Mai Kien?" he asked.

"I am," Mai said. Soldiers often came to the bunk house to collect families when they were approved for travel.

"Follow me," the soldier said. Mai grasped Lang's hand on one side and Tran's on the other. The three of them headed toward the Resettlement office. Tran danced along, trying to escape from Mai's grip. Finally, Mai let go of him to steady Lang as she made her way over tree roots and rocks.

There were several families gathered outside the government building. Mai assumed soldiers had sent for them too. Kids ran around and adults talked animatedly. The atmosphere seemed festive. A woman in a green military jacket and mid-length skirt called Mai's name. Mai grabbed Tran's hand and the three of them entered the building.

"Good news," the woman said, her gaze moving between Lang and Tran. "We processed your papers, and everything is in order."

Mai grinned. "So we are set to go to America. Will we be leaving today?"

The woman frowned. "It's not quite that easy. We are working on finding a sponsor for you and then you'll know where your new home will be," she explained. Mai noticed the woman's voice was soft and she frowned when she mentioned finding a sponsor.

Without a sponsor, a person or group who would find them housing and jobs, the U.S. government wouldn't allow them to come. "How long will that take?" Mai asked.

The woman looked away. "I've been working on that. It isn't easy to find a sponsor for a young woman who has to support both a sister and a child."

Although Mai knew they needed a sponsor, she didn't expect to have trouble finding one. Other refugees seemed to quickly find a sponsor once they were approved for travel. Disappointment made her temper flare. She could feel her cheeks burn and her shoulders tense. "We've been waiting months to go to the United States," she said. "And now you tell me that you can't find a sponsor." She spit each word out in disgust while she waved a fist in the air.

The woman stepped back.

"Every day, we work hard at camp, learning English and doing our jobs. But you are not working hard enough at your job." Mai stepped toward the woman who backed up more.

Lang placed her hands firmly on Mai's shoulders, holding her back. "Mai, we have waited this long. We can wait a while longer."

Just as fast as the white hot anger filled Mai's body, it flowed out. Her shoulders dropped and she exhaled loudly. "I'm sorry," Mai said and then ran from the building. A few minutes later, Lang and Tran caught up to Mai, who was leaning against a tree, crying. During the entire journey, she never cried and now she couldn't stop.

41 ~ Returning to America 2024

Kim's conversation with Aunt Lang about quitting soccer stuck in her mind. For the rest of the day, she lay on the couch, feet propped up on the arm, thoughts banging around in her head like bumper cars.

She couldn't stop thinking about Lang's escape from Vietnam. Leaving your parents and all your special treasures behind to move to the United States must have been so hard. Kim wondered if she could be that brave. And what a surprise that Lang planned to play college soccer in the United States until being shot changed that. Kim felt Aunt Lang's terror and disappointment, but she still couldn't believe Lang gave up. A shiver ran through Kim. Kind of like me giving up, she thought.

When the late afternoon sky turned purple and crimson, the front door opened, and Kim's parents rushed in. Her dad's hair was disheveled, and his shoulders slumped. Her mom looked equally tired, but Grandma Mai walked into the room, taking each step with a happy bounce. Her smooth gray hair was gathered neatly in a bun.

Kim jumped off the couch and flew into her mom's arms. "Mom, Dad, Grandma, I'm sorry I made you come back early." She nuzzled her head in the hollow of her mom's neck, just like she used to do when she was little.

"We were ready to return," Dad said, wrapping an arm around her. "We didn't know if you would still be missing until we saw Lang's text when we landed. I'm relieved you're safe. " His chest rose and fell in a sigh.

Lang appeared in the kitchen doorway with a teapot in her hand. Kim's dad winked at her. Tea signaled a serious discussion. "I want to hear all about your trip and I'm sure Kim needs to talk. Anyone for tea?" Lang asked.

After everyone settled around the kitchen table, Grandma Mai looked at Kim. "I have so many second cousins in Vietnam. Someday, I want you to meet them." Mai radiated joy. Kim was relieved the discussion didn't start with her running away. She just wanted to savor the feeling of her parents sitting near her. She wasn't ready to talk.

Mai took a sip of tea and set the cup down. "Lang, our cousins helped me find Duc. He is married with eleven grandchildren, but he remembered me. We had a wonderful visit." A shadow of sadness appeared on Mai's face, but the joy quickly returned. "I saw Ma and Ba's graves and visited our old home. Lang, we watched a football game on the very field in Vinhomes Central Park where you used to play."

Kim expected Lang to look sad or angry at the mention of Vietnam and football. Instead, Aunt Lang winked at her. Grandma Mai placed her hand over Lang's. "I fell in love with Vietnam again, but I'm at peace with our decision to leave."

"Oh, Grandma, I'm just beginning to understand why you left and why you wanted to return. I want to travel there with you," she said, her eyes meeting Lang's.

"I would like to come as well," Lang said. Grandma Mai's eyebrows arched, and she nodded.

The conversation turned lively, and they kept interrupting each other with laughter and questions. During a break in the conversation, Kim's dad looked at her, the worry lines on his forehead growing deeper. "Are you ready to talk, Kim? Tell us what's going on. Lang told us that you're having trouble with your team. Is that what made you run away?"

"Partly. I was having trouble with some girls on my team." Kim told them about the teasing, the ice cream disaster, the soda being spilled in her lap, and Coach's failed attempt to help. She ended with finding Jayna in the soccer stadium. "It turns out Jayna wants to quit soccer. She's got some things to figure out, but we're friends now." Kim hesitated and looked at Aunt Lang for approval. "But I'm still not sure if I want to play in the Championship tomorrow."

Lang smiled. "If you decide to play, I will be sitting in the stands, cheering you on."

Grandma blinked and her jaw dropped open. Even dad looked stunned. "I feel out of the loop, like we've missed some important things," Dad said, his voice reflecting more of a question than a statement.

Aunt Lang nodded and Kim took it as a signal to tell her parents more. "But there's more to why I ran away. I found a box in the attic that belonged to Aunt Lang and took it without asking. When she got mad, I took off." Kim pointed to a box sitting on the counter.

Grandma Mai stared at the scrapbook and ribbons gathered next to the box on the counter. Her head jerked toward Lang. "Is that your box?"

Aunt Lang nodded before Kim interrupted. "Grandma, there is so much I learned while you were gone. I didn't know that Lang played football." Then she frowned. "I didn't know about your terrible escape from Vietnam. You were so brave."

Mai looked at Lang. "It seems that you and Kim had your own adventure while we were gone."

"I told Kim about escaping from Vietnam on the boat, and I want her to learn more about our eventful trip, but we need to start at the bus station," Lang said.

Mai nodded. "Yes. Our journey from Vietnam started at a bus station. After waiting in the ticket line for hours, soldiers closed the station because the buses were full. After leaving the station, we heard a cry from a small boy hidden in an alley."

Lang picked up the story from placing him in the taxi, to caring for him on the boat, to Mai claiming him as her son in the Indonesian camp. "Kim, that little boy is your dad."

Kim's eyes opened wider. More pieces to the puzzle fit together. "Dad, do you remember being in that alley?"

Her dad shook his head. "I was too young. Until recently, I thought a family friend asked Grandma Mai to take me with her. I do remember playing with kids at the refugee camp in Indonesia and riding a huge plane to the United States."

Kim slipped her hand into her dad's. "I've always known you were adopted, but that's the best adoption story I've ever heard."

Mai abruptly stood and headed toward the stairs. "I just thought of something I'd like to share with you. Be right back." The group sat at the table, her parents excitedly talking about the trip.

A few minutes later, Mai returned with a small leatherbound book in one hand. "After our escape from Vietnam, a very special friend gave me this journal. He told me to write down everything that happened to me because someday my family would want to know. Nobody knew I kept this journal and wrote in it for years."

Grandma Mai handed the journal to Kim. "To practice my English, I rewrote each entry in the back of the journal. It is yours to read now." The journal was held closed by two black elastic bands. "When you have questions as you read, come to me. In this family, there will be no more secrets."

Mom, Dad, and Grandma said they were tired after the long day of travel from Vietnam. Soon after their conversation at the kitchen table, her parents grabbed their suitcases and left for their own house. Kim followed, holding the journal to her chest as if it were a precious jewel.

Evening turned to night and Kim tried to sleep, but stories from Aunt Lang and Grandma Mai replayed in her head like a movie. She still had so many questions. Sitting up in bed and turning on a light, Kim opened the journal and began to read. As the sky turned from inky black to pinkish gray right before dawn, she finished the journal and fell asleep.

42 ~ Going to America 1978

"Lang. Tran! Hurry up. We're going to be late," Mai called from inside the bunkhouse. She tucked her journal under her pillow and headed out the door.

Tran followed, clutching the tiny wooden boat he got from Duc. "Ma, I'm taking my boat with me. It is just like the boat we took from Vietnam."

Mai's heart swelled with pride. Tran was bright, cheerful, and resilient. It was only six months since they arrived in Indonesia, but he only remembered a few details from their week-long escape on the fishing boat from Vietnam. For Tran, it was a great adventure. Memories of gunshots, pirates, and the typhoon were forgotten.

Lang limped out of the bunkhouse next. "I'm ready." After arriving in Indonesia, Lang immersed herself in learning English at the camp school. To Mai, it was hard to tell if Lang was happy. She seemed content but refused to do the exercises the doctor showed her to make her leg stronger. She walked away if anyone mentioned football and went out of her way to avoid walking by the makeshift football field at the camp. Of course, Lang never brought up the shooting.

Mai started down the path with the others following behind her. One day each week for months, they walked to the government office to check if they had a sponsor yet. Each week, the same woman shuffled through the piles of paperwork on her desk and said, "No."

"Why do you keep going?" Lang asked. "Every week, we get up early and walk to the government office, only to be told there isn't any news. Why don't you just wait until they come to you?"

Mai sighed and looked at Tran, who was making his boat sail across an imaginary ocean as they walked. "If I show up every week, they won't forget me. It reminds them to keep working on finding us a sponsor."

When the three of them walked into the government office, the woman was standing there, smiling, and holding a piece of paper above her head as if it were a trophy. "You have a sponsor. A church in a small town near Milwaukee, Wisconsin, has an apartment and a job in a pharmacy set up for you. You will leave tomorrow."

Mai's head spun. "What about Lang and Tran?"

"They are working on enrolling Lang in high school and a woman from the church will take care of Tran while you work."

Milwaukee? Wisconsin? Mai walked over to a large map thumbtacked to the wall and studied it. The woman followed and planted her index finger next to a city near the top of the map. "Milwaukee is next to a very big lake. I know you were hoping for San Francisco, but the lake will make it feel a bit like home."

Mai smiled and shrugged. How could she be disappointed when they were going to the United States. If they didn't like Milwaukee, they could eventually move. She grabbed Tran's and Lang's hands, and they did a little celebration dance. "We are going to America!"

43 ~ A New Beginning 2024

The sun blazed across the room, forcing Kim to throw the blanket off. It felt like she just fell asleep. The journal was too interesting to put down last night, and through Grandma's eyes, she felt like she was part of their journey. Kim's phone vibrated and she grabbed it to look at the text.

"1:00 game 2day. Plz come. lmk."

She decided to ignore the text from Jayna for now. Jayna said she was quitting soccer so why would she care if Kim came? Hopping out of bed, she put on her soccer uniform, and tramped downstairs.

Her mom and dad sat at the kitchen table drinking coffee. "Hello, sleepyhead," Mom teased. "Would you like breakfast or lunch?"

Kim sat down at the table. "Lunch, I guess."

Dad looked up from his phone. "So, you're going to play in the championship today?"

Kim shrugged. "I think so. Jayna texted asking me to come." They were quiet for a moment. "I read Grandma's journal last night. Did you know you spent months in Indonesia after leaving Vietnam? That a church right here in Wisconsin sponsored Grandma Mai so all of you could come to the U.S.? Do you remember moving here?"

Kim's dad leaned back in his chair. He pinched the bridge of his nose and looked deep in thought. "It was so long ago," he finally said. "I remember the plane ride to the United States with other refugees and living in a tiny apartment. It was confusing because I couldn't speak English."

Mom set a grilled cheese sandwich, grapes, and carrot sticks in front of Kim. "Eat. You need to leave soon."

Kim talked while she ate. "Dad, I admire Grandma Mai and Aunt Lang. They moved to a country where they didn't know anyone and didn't speak English. Lang went to school and watched you after school. Grandma worked long hours in a pharmacy until she saved enough money to open her own store. In Vietnam, people who used to be their friends bullied Grandma and Aunt Lang, and some neighbors here didn't make them feel welcome either."

Kim's dad put his cup of coffee down. "Ah ha!" he said. "That's why you decided to play soccer today."

Kim nodded. "If Grandma Mai and Aunt Lang handled the hate, I can too." Kim grabbed her duffel bag containing her soccer cleats and filled her water bottle.

Dad gave her a hug. "Mom and I will take you to the game. We can't wait to see you play. We're proud of you." He got his car keys and Mom grabbed her purse. Then they were off.

When Kim arrived at the soccer field, the other players were already warming up. Her stomach clenched into a tight ball, and she wasn't sure if she wanted to get out of the car. Her dad put the car in park. "You've got this, Kim."

Her voice shook. "Now that I'm here, I'm not so sure. Aunt Lang said she wasn't brave enough to play soccer in the United States. I want to be brave for her, but …"

Kim's mom turned toward the back seat. "You said that Lang regretted not trying. If you choose to leave, will you have that same regret?"

Slowly, Kim's hand inched toward the door handle. She put the strap of the duffel bag over her shoulder and got out of the car. Walking toward the bench, Kim saw Jayna sitting next to Coach Tim. She was wearing shorts and a t-shirt instead of her soccer uniform. When Coach saw Kim, he waved her over. "Jayna told me she hasn't made things easy for you the last few months. I didn't realize how bad things were."

Kim looked gratefully at Jayna. It must have been hard for her to come today and tell Coach Tim about the awful things she did. "Coach, I didn't tell you everything because I thought Jayna would make things worse if you talked to her."

Coach Tim winced. "I'm sorry, Kim. You told me you were having problems with Jayna. It was my job as the coach to step in and I didn't do that."

She didn't blame him. She didn't want Coach to step in, but would the bullying have been that bad if she talked to him earlier? Then maybe neither of them would have run away. "If I had it to do over again, I would've asked you for help," Kim said quietly.

She watched the girls warming up on the field, and all the bad feelings returned. "Coach, I'm sorry I skipped practices, and I didn't trust you to help me. Can I still play in the championship today?"

Coach Tim placed a hand on Kim's shoulder. "Of course. I was hoping you would come today."

Kim felt grateful that Coach was giving her another chance. "But, I'm worried about how the girls will treat me."

Coach Tim looked at Jayna and nodded. Jayna looked down, a red blush creeping up her cheeks. "I felt awful, so I sent a group text to the team, asking them to come early. When they got here, I talked to Coach Tim and the team. Please play today." She picked up a soccer ball and tossed it to Kim. Then Jayna walked off the field.

Coach smiled at Kim. "I'm glad you're back. The team needs you."

Kim nodded and jogged onto the field. Some girls looked away, but some shouted words of encouragement. Stella gave her a thumbs up. Fifteen minutes into the game, Kim's misgivings vanished. They treated her like part of the team, passing the ball to her when she was in the right position and giving high-fives when she made a great play.

The first half ended and the team, ahead 2-1, ran across the field to get a drink. Kim looked into the stands as she headed to the bench, and suddenly stopped. Her feet stayed planted on the field while the other girls ran past.

Her mom and dad sat in the front row of the bleachers, waving at her and smiling, as usual, but now Grandma Mai and Aunt Lang were beside her dad, holding their fists in the air and chanting, "Go, Kim." Charlotte and Mason hung over the fence in front of the bleachers, waving to Kim.

What astounded Kim the most was the group in the second row. Jayna and her parents were waving and calling her name. Everyone is here to support me, Kim thought. She grinned and the tight feeling in her stomach completely disappeared.

On the sidelines between halves, Kim rested on the bench and Stella sat down beside her. She broke off a piece of her protein bar and handed it to Kim. "I'm sorry for the way I treated you. I was afraid that if I didn't do what Jayna said, she would turn on me too. Everyone else feels the same way but are too embarrassed to say anything."

Kim was grateful for Stella's apology. "I get it. I didn't stand up to Jayna either."

Amira plopped down on the other side of Kim. "I can't believe how I treated you. I'm really sorry." She looked down. "Friends?"

Kim smiled. "Friends."

The ref blew her whistle, and the team ran out on the field. The rest of the game moved quickly with Kim doing a perfect outside kick to assist in a goal. A few minutes later, Stella scored the winning goal. Cheers and applause rained down on the team as they accepted the trophy. Afterwards, Kim ran over to the bleachers. "I can't believe you're all here." She felt embarrassed and ecstatic at the same time.

The group all began talking at once, stopped, and then burst out in laughter. Kim was laughing the hardest. "Jayna, I never thought I would see you in a soccer stadium again."

"I'm not playing soccer anymore," Jayna said, "but after I told my parents how awful I'd been to you, they wanted to come here to cheer you on."

Kim reached over and hugged Jayna. Then Kim turned to Lang. "You came," she whispered. "That must have been so hard."

Aunt Lang's lips turned up in a tentative smile and Grandma Mai wrapped an arm around Lang and grinned. "I told myself that if you could return to the soccer field, then I could too," Lang said.

The serious moment was over, and the group began talking all at once. Two teammates walked by. "Are you coming?" they asked. Kim grinned at her parents. "Mom, Dad, the team decided to go out for pizza. Can we all go?" Kim linked arms with Grandma Mai and Aunt Lang, and they walked to the car together.

44 ~ A New Beginning 1978

Mai, Lang, and Tran hurried back to the bunk house, each carrying a new backpack the woman at the government office gave them. During their stay at Galang camp, Mai bought Lang, Tran, and herself a few changes of clothes and toiletries, but that's all they had. They placed their meager belongings in their backpacks and the packing was done.

While Lang and Tran went outside to say goodbye to the friends they made at the camp, Mai slid the small journal Duc gave her from under her pillow and began writing about her last day at Galang camp. She wrote about sweet, friendly Tran, who was now her son. How could he be so well-adjusted and happy when he never knew a life with a mom, dad, or home? She wrote about Lang's carefree days playing football in Vietnam and how she lost confidence and joy after being shot. Would Lang ever return to that active, hopeful teenager?

Finally, she wrote about how much she loved her new little family. If they survived a terrifying boat trip to Indonesia and a crowded refugee camp, she was confident they could survive anything. Mai stuffed the journal deep into her backpack before going to her final shift at work.

* **

In the morning, Mai, Lang and Tran joined a group of refugees outside the bunkhouse and they walked down the narrow path to the beach. The journey would begin by boarding a ferry to Singapore where they would board a plane to Los Angeles, and then from there, fly to Milwaukee. At the beach, the ferry bobbed alongside the dock. Although it was a ferry instead of a small fishing boat, Mai's heart fluttered, and she saw Lang's mouth quiver. The ride would only take an hour, but it would be their first time at sea since their escape from Vietnam.

Mai reached out for Lang's hand, and they boarded together. Settling into a plastic seat, Mai momentarily squeezed her eyes shut, trying to block out memories of storms and pirate attacks. Lang sat rigidly beside her. Tran skipped up and down the aisle, grinning as he clutched his little wooden boat. She was thankful he was excited about the trip instead of scared.

The trip to Milwaukee was long, more than twenty-four exhausting hours. They were tired and hungry when they exited the plane at Milwaukee's Mitchell Field Airport and walked down the jet bridge. She glanced at Lang, whose pupils were huge. Again, they clasped their hands.

Mai looked up and saw a group of at least 20 people holding signs and balloons. They were waving their arms at her and cheering. Although Mai was just beginning to learn English, she could read the words "Mai, Lang & Tran - Welcome to the U.S.A."

Holding Lang's hand on her left and Tran's on her right, Mai walked toward the crowd. She was so tired, and the noise of voices around her overwhelmed her. With a weary smile, she turned toward the people holding the signs and bowed her head slightly. "Hello, I am Mai." Lang stood behind Mai but bowed her head as well. Tran gleefully shrieked while trying to catch a big red balloon. Several people laughed.

A young woman, with golden hair and a wide smile, stepped forward and put out her hand. "Welcome to Wisconsin. We're glad you're here." Mai grasped the warm hand and felt a surge of hope. Although she was thousands of miles from Vietnam, Mai felt like she was home.

45 ~ Full Circle
2024

After a pizza celebration, the Kien family returned home. Grandma Mai arrived home a few minutes before Kim's parents and was waiting in her front yard when they pulled in. Mai waved Kim over. She hopped out of the car and followed Grandma Mai into the house.

Lang sat in her usual spot on the couch, knitting, but smiled at Kim. "I think that was the most fun I've had in years. It felt so good to be at a soccer field, even if I was just a spectator.

"Grandma and Aunt Lang, it meant so much to me that you came. Will you watch some of my games next year?"

Lang nodded. "We would love to."

Grandma Mai sat down on the other end of the couch and motioned for Kim to sit between them. "My journal told most of our story," she began. "But there is more. Your great-grandparents raised Lang and me to be strong independent women. That was unusual in Vietnam forty years ago. You would have loved Ma."

Kim noticed that Grandma looked sad. "Why didn't they come with you?"

Grandma Mai sighed. "Ma had a heart condition and was too weak to travel. They were going to join us later, but life in Vietnam was difficult and Ma died before they were able to come. Ba was too heartbroken to leave after that."

Reaching under the neckline of her tunic, Grandma pulled out a golden heart that hung from a fine golden chain. Reaching behind her neck, she unhooked the clasp and placed it in the palm of Kim's hand. The heart sparkled in the evening sunlight that peeked through the window.

Kim was familiar with the chain. For as long as she could remember, the chain hung around Grandma's neck and disappeared under the silk tunics she wore. When she asked about it, Grandma Mai always changed the subject. This was the first time Kim saw the heart.

"My mother gave this to me right before Lang and I left for the bus station. The circle slipping from the end of the heart symbolizes family circling around each other in support. She said to hold it in my hand when life gets tough, and it would give me courage. When Lang was injured or had trouble adjusting to life in Wisconsin, I gave it to her to hold. Life has been tough for you lately. It is time for you to wear the necklace." Aunt Lang nodded in agreement.

Kim stared at the delicate golden heart, the chain snaking between her fingers. The heart felt warm, like a gentle squeeze from a friend. She looked at Grandma Mai, feeling grateful and loved. "Thank you," she said softly.

"There's more. Kim, your name has a special meaning in Vietnamese. It means gold," Grandma continued. "The necklace is made from precious gold, and you are more precious than gold to all of us."

Grandma Mai took the necklace and fastened it around Kim's neck. Kim wrapped her arms around Grandma in a hug, the necklace fitting snugly between them.

About the Author

Kelly Flanagan was an award-winning elementary school teacher. She was selected for Wisconsin's Herb Kohl award for outstanding educators and was National Board Certified in middle grades. She has a B.S. in Journalism and a Master of Education.

As a 4th/5th grade teacher, Kelly's passion was running lively book group discussions with her students. She believes there are no reluctant readers — just kids who haven't found a book they love yet. Her goal is to write that book. Kelly is awed by people brave enough to upend their lives to move to a new country. Her new novel, *Holding Onto Courage,* highlights that bravery and sense of adventure.

Kelly lives in Oconomowoc, Wisconsin with her husband. In the winter, she can be found in Florida's panhandle, walking the white sand beaches. Besides writing, Kelly tutors low income students, spends time with her four active grandchildren, and plays hours of pickleball.

Follow Kelly at www.kellyflanagan.me

ALL THINGS THAT MATTER PRESS

FOR MORE INFORMATION ON TITLES AVAILABLE FROM
ALL THINGS THAT MATTER PRESS, GO TO
http://allthingsthatmatterpress.com
or contact us at
allthingsthatmatterpress@gmail.com

**If you enjoyed this book, please post a review on Amazon.com and your favorite social media sites.
Thank you!**

www.ingramcontent.com/pod-product-compliance
Lightning Source LLC
LaVergne TN
LVHW050550160826
845677LV00011B/2251

* 9 7 9 8 9 9 1 5 3 7 2 2 3 *